ROOM

KENDALL RYAN

The Room Mate
Copyright © 2017 Kendall Ryan

Copy Editing by
Pam Berehulke

Cover Design by
Sara Eirew

Photography by
Brian Jamie

Cover Model
Christian Hogue

About the Book

The last time I saw my best friend's younger brother, he was a geek wearing braces. But when Cannon shows up to crash in my spare room, I get a swift reality check.

Now twenty-four, he's broad shouldered and masculine, and so sinfully sexy, I want to climb him like the jungle gyms we used to enjoy. At six-foot-something with lean muscles hiding under his T-shirt, a deep sexy voice, and full lips that pull into a smirk when he studies me, he's pure temptation.

Fresh out of a messy breakup, he doesn't want any entanglements. But I can resist, right?

I'm holding strong until the third night of our new arrangement when we get drunk and he confesses his biggest secret of all: he's cursed when it comes to sex. Apparently he's a god in bed, and women instantly fall in love with him.

I'm calling bullshit. In fact, I'm going to prove him wrong, and if I rack up a few much-needed orgasms in the process, all the better.

There's no way I'm going to fall in love with Cannon. But once we start . . . I realize betting against him may have been the biggest mistake of my life.

Prologue

Looking back over the last two months, I could only wonder how I came to be standing over his body holding a can of gasoline and a book of matches.

This wasn't me, wasn't the path my life was supposed to go down, and yet here I was—entangled with a man who would never be mine, and staring into the face of what was surely a class-A felony.

Love makes you do crazy, irrational things. And yet, even knowing where we'd end up, I doubted I would have had the strength to stop myself from falling for him. There was just something about him that called to me. Something magnetic and primal.

Looking down at his still form, I yearned for him even now. I sure as hell picked a weird moment to decide I loved him.

The powerful stench of gasoline hit my nostrils, pulling me from my daydream. It was time to move.

Chapter One

Cannon

The heart was a strange and amazing muscle. You couldn't live or love without it, but most people didn't think about it often. Didn't think about the steady, faithful organ that beat one hundred thousand times a day. Most people probably didn't know that a woman's heartbeat was faster than a man's by about eight beats per minute, or that its four chambers pumped blood to every cell in the body except for the corneas.

Yet it could be a pesky little nuisance at times. Making us feel things we didn't want to, say and do things we'd never planned on. And lately, it was the source of all my problems. But at this exact moment, the heart wasn't what I was concerned with. It was a body part further south, much further south.

I liked vaginas. I really did. But staring into the mouth of one old enough to belong to my grandmother wasn't my idea of an exciting evening. *No fucking thank you.*

"Everything looks good, Mrs. Thurston." Snapping off my latex gloves, I rose to my feet, threw them in the trash, then helped her into a sitting position on the exam table.

She adjusted her bifocals and offered me a coy smile. "Thank you for making that so pleasant. There should be a new rule that all gynecologists have to look like you."

I chuckled. "Thank you. But I'm not a gynecologist. I'm a med student on my OB-GYN rotation."

That ends tomorrow, thank God. I've been inside more vaginas these last four weeks than all four years of undergrad combined. And that's saying something, believe me.

But this rotation would be the closest I'd get to any pussy for a good long while. I'd sworn a temporary ban three days ago, after my latest fling went psycho.

Her wild streak in bed had made her an excellent fuck-buddy, but apparently that extra dose of crazy ran deeper than I thought. She swore we were soul mates, yet I didn't even know her last name or which sports teams she rooted for. I told her what we'd shared the past few weeks was fun, but that it was over.

Two days later, my place was broken into and nearly everything I owned was destroyed. Bleach was poured over my couch, bed, and clothes, and my laptop and TV smashed. She was currently in police custody, and I'd been crashing on a friend's couch while I tried to figure out my next move. My landlord had decided I was too much trouble and served me an eviction notice. Working twelve-hour shifts didn't exactly allow much time for house-hunting.

Dick, *good dick*, made women crazy. It turned women's hearts into a frenzied mess, causing them to declare their undying love and latch on. I couldn't continue to unleash that kind of chaos. I needed to buckle down and focus on my education and my future. I had to declare my specialty and apply for residencies for next year, and I was already pushing the deadline as it was. My mother and older sister were counting on me. They were what really mattered, not chasing women. It was a no-brainer. My nights inside the silky-warm perfection of a woman's most tender place were done.

Until I graduated and landed a job, anyway.

Mom and Allie had sacrificed too much. I'd worked too hard, winning scholarships and keeping my grades up. I couldn't lose it all now . . . and I had the sinking feeling that that was exactly what might happen. My nose had spent too much time sniffing out pussy and not enough on the grindstone. Sure, thinking with my dick had been fun while it lasted, but it wasn't worth losing everything. Now I had to buckle down, put my Ivy League education to good use, and hope it wasn't already too late.

Yep . . . the new Cannon Roth was going to be levelheaded, in control, and most importantly: *celibate*. I'd just have to settle for swabbing the insides of seventy-year-olds like Mrs. Thurston with a giant Q-tip. Not nearly as satisfying, but it was about to become my way of life.

Sitting down on the stool across from my patient, I typed a few notes into the laptop. "If only all patients could be as easy as you, Mrs. Thurston."

"Did you just call me easy?" She winked.

"I did have my hand up your skirt after barely a hello." I grinned back at her.

The attending physician's eyes widened but Mrs. Thurston merely laughed, a deep, throaty sound that made me grin.

"Thank you for that." She reached one wrinkled, age-spotted hand toward me, and when I placed my hand in hers, she squeezed. "I haven't had a doctor take the time to treat me like a regular person in a long time. You'll make a great physician one day."

I accepted her compliment with a smile. It wasn't the first time I'd been told my bedside manner put people at ease. And if I couldn't have fun with my patients, there was no way I'd survive the twelve-hour shifts and lack of sleep. It could be brutal sometimes.

As I walked into the hall after Dr. Haslett, he said something about running cultures for a preventive screening, and I nodded. Then a cute nurse winked at me, her gaze dropping to the front of my scrubs where I was certain the outline of my dick had her mouth

watering. I was two seconds away from leading her

into the storage room for a quick fuck when my brain snapped into action.

Shit. I'd made my celibacy vow not even five minutes ago and was already tempted to break it. What had I been thinking? Clearly this idea was doomed to fail . . . which meant I needed a replacement. Something I could actually stick to. I smiled and walked straight past the nurse as I started concocting a new plan in my head.

There would be three simple rules to follow if I needed to get laid. It could only last one night, no names would be exchanged, and no phone numbers either. Following those rules ensured it would be a one-time thing, and the woman couldn't go falling in love with me after. That meant no fucking the pretty nurses at the hospital where I worked.

Feeling the tiniest bit more in control, I rolled my shoulders and checked my watch. Still two more hours until my twelve-hour shift ended.

Just then, my phone vibrated. I reached into my pocket and skimmed the screen as I continued following Dr. Haslett to our next appointment. It was a text from

Allie, telling me she'd found me a place to live.

I smiled with relief. Thank God, at least one of my problems was solved . . .

Then I finished reading her message.

My smile crashed to the floor. Allie wanted me to share a house with Paige, her oldest and closest friend. Her hot-as-hell, totally off-limits BFF who I'd lusted after from the moment I hit puberty.

The gods had just laughed at my plan and thrown a curveball of their own. Something told me I was about to become very well-acquainted with my hand.

Chapter Two

Paige

At twenty-eight, a woman began to question things. Big, complex things like destiny, fate, and what I was supposed to be doing with my life. I was fairly certain my grand purpose didn't include working fifty hours a week and never experiencing anything more exciting than splurging on spicy Thai takeout every Friday night. Surely there had to be more to life than that.

But lately life had been like a cheap pair of underwear—sneaking up, surprising you with discomfort at all the worst times.

Little did I know that destiny was about to smack me in the face with her irony.

My phone rang, and I grabbed it from the counter. "Hello?"

"I need your help, Paige," my best friend said as soon as I answered.

Abandoning the stack of junk mail I'd been

flipping through, I leaned against the dining table. Enchilada was snoring underneath it, dreaming about whatever tiny dogs dream about.

"Sure, Allie. What's going on?"

She hesitated, making me wonder what kind of favor she had in mind. Allie was like a sister to me; she had to know there wasn't anything I wouldn't do for her.

"Cannon needs a place to stay," she finally said.

Except for that.

Suppressing a sudden twitch in my jaw, I slipped off my heels and took a sip from my water bottle. Cannon? Share my tiny place with her geeky little brother who I hadn't seen or spoken to in years? Awkward much?

I was a private person, and I valued my alone time. It was why I chose to have no roommates and no drama. This was not the news I wanted on a Thursday evening after a hectic day at work. Allie, Cannon, and I had been pretty much inseparable growing up, but after we'd moved on and left for college, I hadn't kept in touch with him at all.

"I don't know, Allie. My place is pretty tight as it is." I lived in a six-hundred-square-foot duplex, and while I did technically have a spare room, its only furnishings were a lumpy futon and a writing desk. Just thinking about sharing this sardine can with another person made me feel stuffy, so I wandered into the living room to open the window. "Why can't he stay with you and James?"

Allie hesitated for a beat, and I knew I wouldn't like her answer. "James doesn't think that's a good idea. He and I have only just started living together. It's a big step, you know?"

Funny how your decisions as a couple seem to line up with his wants more often than yours. It was just another reason on the growing list of why I didn't like her new fiancé. But I didn't want to get back into *that* swamp of a conversation again, so I merely offered a noncommittal grunt.

As she kept trying to persuade me, I idly watched a man approach along the sidewalk leading to my house. I lived in half of an old Victorian house a few blocks from the University of Michigan campus, so I was sure his destination wasn't actually *my* house, but a girl could dream. Dressed in a black V-neck sweater, dark jeans, and boots, he was tall and muscular. His messy hair was cropped neatly on the sides, but long enough on top to grab during rough sex and hang onto for what would surely be the ride of my life.

I shook my head, shocked at my suddenly dirty mind. *What the hell?* Where had that thought come from? Lack of sex and being overworked, most likely. I pushed the thought away and tried to pay attention.

"His apartment was ransacked, and he's basically homeless," Allie was explaining, her tone pleading.

"I'll think about it," I said, trying to stand my ground.

The guy outside stopped in front of my house and studied the house numbers. In my spot from the second-story front window, I stayed mostly concealed, peeking out from behind the heavy drapes.

Now that he was closer, I could make out green eyes fringed in thick black lashes, and a five o'clock shadow on his square jaw. He was perfection.

His mouth was etched into a firm line, his expression impassive. If you were going to get a read on this man, first you were going to have to work to get beneath his steely reserve.

"He's in his last year of med school, and in just over two months, he'll be moving away for a residency. It'd be stupid for him to sign a new lease. Please, Paige?"

Ugh. All right, already. I swore I could hear her puppy-dog eyes over the phone.

"Fine. Two months."

Allie squealed her thanks, but I wasn't listening anymore. Those long legs had started carrying the man forward again, and this time, right up my front steps.

Shit! He was headed for my door. My heart pounded faster, and my mouth went totally dry.

"I have to go, Allie."

"Thanks, Paigey! I owe you one," she sang.

I tossed my phone on the coffee table and hurried toward the door. As I went, I snatched a glance of myself in the hall mirror, and was relieved to see that I still looked pulled together from work. Black pencil skirt, white silk blouse, my blond hair tied into a long ponytail.

The confident series of knocks on my front door made my stomach flutter. My fingers curled around the doorknob and when I pulled it open, my breath caught at what I saw. If I thought he was merely attractive before, nothing could have prepared me for having him so close. He towered over me—at least six foot three, I'd wager—and had a muscular build that advertised hours of dedication at the gym. His scent was maddening. It wasn't cologne. It was subtler than that, maybe bodywash, but it was crisp and masculine and mouthwatering nonetheless.

"Paige?" he asked.

Shit, even his voice was hot, deep and smooth and rich.

More importantly, Mister Sex-on-Legs knew my name.

I squinted at him, my mouth opening, then closing without a sound. Recognition clawed at the edges of my brain.

"C-Cannon?" I forced out, my voice breathless and thick.

His mouth pulled into a happy smirk, and he held out a hand. "God, it's been years."

"At least five," I said, placing my palm in his. His hand was warm and solid, and the touch of his skin sent tingles rushing through me. My nipples hardened into points beneath my bra, and my ovaries did a little happy dance. It had been months since I'd had a man in my house, and my entire body was primed and ready.

"You look well," he said, still smirking at me. And still clasping my hand.

"You've grown up," was all I managed. Holy hell, had he ever.

He'd gone away to college at Yale, where he'd finished early, then moved to Pennsylvania for med school. He'd transferred to Michigan at some point last year, although I wasn't clear on why. Allie occasionally gave me updates about his life, but he and I weren't close anymore, not like when we were kids. He was her kid brother; I had no reason to know the intimate details about him. But standing before him now at the threshold of my small home, something felt very intimate about this moment.

"So have you." His gaze traced down the length of me, pausing briefly at my breasts—which had never been more achy and full. I suppressed a flash of disappointment when he finally dropped my hand.

The fuck . . . this was Cannon. And here he was staring at my breasts. My brain struggled to catch up to what was happening.

He'd always been somewhat serious. In high school, he'd preferred science over field parties, and was more comfortable as captain of the debate team than he ever would have been as captain of the football team. He was intelligent and curious, and made no apologies about his interests. Not that being a little different had hurt him any in the popularity department. He was the type to easily move between social circles, hanging out with the nerds and the jocks alike. But he'd clearly grown into his own man since the last time I saw him.

He might be young, twenty-four years to my twenty-eight, but his eyes spoke of wisdom and maturity. This new Cannon was civilized and sharp-witted. Cultured and dashingly handsome. I couldn't quite put my finger on what had changed, though his physical presence was a large part of it.

Just standing near him made my heart pick up its pace. My fingertips tingled with the desire to reach out and touch him. *Seriously, what the hell is happening to me?* This was Cannon freaking Roth. Soon to be *Dr.* Cannon Roth. That had a yummy ring to it.

Shaking my head against the rush of desire to play doctor with him, I scolded myself. He was Allie's brother, which meant he was practically family. And Allie would kick my ass if anything happened between us. She'd always been a mother hen, and although she was fiercely overprotective of everyone she cared about, her precious baby brother got the brunt of it.

"I know you spoke with Allie, but I wanted to come by myself and make sure you were comfortable with this."

Just the act of standing near him made my mind wander to things like sheet-clawing sex, the smell of latex, and regrets the morning after.

My best friend's little brother wasn't so little anymore. And he'd just marched into my life, turning my girly bits into warm, aroused mush.

Fuck!

"Of course," I lied.

Chapter Three

Cannon

Paige was lying.

There was something about having me here that made her uncomfortable. Perhaps it was the strong physical attraction I could feel radiating between us. Her scent was intoxicating, light and feminine and delicate. I didn't have time for distractions, and I'd just promised myself there would be no more fucking around. But all of that went out the window the second I laid eyes on Paige.

The stolen sight of her tits when I was fourteen had inspired a lifelong love affair with breasts. Her honey-colored hair was the reason I'd always preferred blondes. And while I'd caught glimpses of her on my sister's social media over the years, in person she was . . . *wow.*

"Come inside," she said, opening the door wider.

I obeyed and followed her in.

Now that I was here in her space, watching her subtle reaction to me and feeling her discomfort, I wanted to flee.

I hadn't seen Paige in years, and fuck if she hadn't grown up into a beautiful woman. Toned legs beneath a fitted skirt, the tempting curve of a round ass, the soft swell of breasts hidden behind a silky top.

I'd had more dirty fantasies about her while growing up than I'd ever admit. She was my sister's best friend, which meant she'd slept over at our house hundreds of times, gone swimming with us dozens. As a child, I'd chased behind her and my sister on my bike, and cried when they refused to hang out with me. As a teenager, even though I spent less time trailing after my sister and more around my own friends, Paige was never far from my brain.

All my raging hormones overflowed straight onto her. I'd hear her giggling through the wall of Allie's room as they talked about boys, and wish I could make her laugh like that, *be* one of the boys she wanted. The sight of her in a swimsuit or a tank top or even a tight pair of jeans had never failed to give me an instant boner. Watching movies together on the couch, I had ached to touch her knee or press my thigh against hers, but I could only sit paralyzed with nervous need— and bite Allie's head off when she inevitably teased me for being so quiet.

When Allie suggested I stay here for the rest of the semester, my cock had twitched with interest. Clearly those old, secret fantasies had only slept, never died. But nothing could have prepared me for actually being here, watching Paige's pulse thrum in her throat, smelling her warm, feminine scent, feeling her reaction to me. Now a grown man, I knew the effect I had on women. I was tall, well-groomed, and never failed to turn a few heads. But this was Paige . . . I shouldn't want this, right?

"Who's this?" I asked, grinning down at the tiny pup at her ankles.

Paige looked down as if she hadn't noticed the overgrown rat running up to us. "This is Enchilada," she said almost defensively.

Weird-ass name for a dog, but who was I to judge? Maybe she was a Mexican food enthusiast.

She reached down and lifted the dog with one hand under his belly and held him at her side, stroking his fur with the other hand.

"So did Allie just spring this on you, or were you okay with the idea?" I asked, wondering how honest she'd be.

"She actually just called me when you were walking up." Paige blushed a little at the admission, but I had no idea why she should feel embarrassed about that.

Dammit, Allie. My big sister could be so absentminded sometimes. But I guessed Paige knew that as well as I did, and we loved her anyway.

"So you're between apartments?" Paige asked, setting the dog down beside us, where he sat with a huff.

I nodded, not wanting to advertise the fact that my ex had destroyed my place. A long history of unstable ex-lovers probably wasn't a desired trait in a roommate.

"It's just that, well, my place is pretty small . . ." She trailed off, her hands clasped together.

She had neatly manicured fingernails, painted light blue. In fact, all of her was neatly groomed, from her long shiny hair that I wanted to wrap around my fist to her full pink lips that I wanted to see around my cock, pulling me deep into her warm mouth. I knew I was supposed to be taking a break from sex, but she made me want to throw out all my rules and say *fuck it*.

"I get it." I stuck my hands in my pockets and rocked back on my heels. "We haven't seen each other in a long time. Living together would be awkward."

She chewed on her lower lip, looking unsure and totally delectable. I'd meant to give her an out if she wanted one, but instead Paige shook her head, resolution flashing on her features.

"I'm sorry. I'm being rude. If you need a place to crash, of course you're welcome."

"Only if you're sure it's no trouble."

Paige cleared her throat. "It's no trouble. Let me show you around."

I nodded and followed her into the combination living/dining room. She had one couch and an armchair, both upholstered in tan microfiber, and two end tables. A pile of throw pillows in creams and blues lay heaped on the couch, and framed black-and-white nature photographs lined the wall opposite the windows. The other end of the room held a round glass dining table and two tufted chairs. Overall, it was small but cozy.

The narrow kitchen wasn't anything fancy, but it was clean and organized. She opened the door to the pantry and said she'd clear off some shelf space for whatever groceries I wanted.

Along a short hallway, there was only one bathroom with a glass stand-up shower stall, and then two bedrooms. Paige's room was the larger of the two, and when I entered, the wood floor creaked under my feet. Her bed was pristinely made with a gray duvet and pale pink sheets with a geometric print, little matching throw pillows piled on top. A bedside table held a stack of books and a reading lamp. The door to her closet stood open, revealing rows and rows of work clothes hung neatly inside.

"Nice place," I commented, following her out into

the hall once again.

"This is the guest room." Paige pushed open a door to reveal a space barely large enough for a bed. It currently held a futon and a writing desk shoved into the corner.

"I'm sorry, I know it's not much—" she started.

"This is perfect. I'm doing my rotation, so I practically live at United Methodist. All I really need at home is a bed." I'd barely even eaten in my last apartment—I scarfed down most of my meals at the hospital cafeteria. I turned my gaze from the room back to Paige. "You probably won't see much of me."

She nodded. "I'm generally home from work by five thirty, and sometimes I walk home for lunch."

Enchilada, who had followed us, sneezed and shook himself with a jingle of silver dog tags. She reached down to lift the pile of light brown and gray fur into her arms again.

I stopped beside the front door, looking down at a pair of pink women's running shoes with orange laces.

"I have a spare key I can leave you. When were you thinking of . . ." Paige shifted beside me, looking uncomfortable again.

"Moving in?"

She nodded.

"Tonight, if you don't mind. I've been couch surfing for the last few nights, staying with buddies around campus."

A quiet, strangled noise escaped her, but she nodded. "Sure."

"I lost pretty much everything, so I really need to run to the store tonight and get some essentials. Might take me a few hours. Are you okay leaving the door unlocked if I promise to be back by ten?"

She nodded. "Of course. I'll see you later."

Something told me this new arrangement was going to test all of my boundaries and then some.

Chapter Four

Paige

After I showed him out the door, I placed my hand against my hammering heart, wondering what in the hell just happened. How I went from spending a quiet evening alone to preparing for a new roommate was beyond me. And not just any roommate, but my best friend's sexy, off-limits brother . . . Cannon freaking Roth.

Pulling a deep breath into my lungs, I shook the thoughts away. I might be attracted to him, but there was no way I'd ever allow myself to act on it. So it didn't matter how handsome he was, how dominating and sexy. I would just have to keep a calm, cool, reasonable head and make the best of these next two months. Well, that, and buy some extra batteries for my trusty BOB.

I found myself walking down the hall to the guest room I'd shown Cannon just minutes before. All that separated this room from mine was a thin wall. I wondered if I'd be able to hear him when he jerked off.

Would he bring girls home and fuck them while I was forced to listen, alone in my bed? I could institute a "no sex allowed" rule to ensure that there'd be no awkward hookups to endure. Only if I did that, he'd find some way to spin it around on me—say it was because I was jealous.

Maybe I hadn't thought this roommate thing through well enough.

Heading toward the kitchen, I grabbed the half-full bottle of chardonnay from the door of my fridge and poured myself a glass. Bringing it to my lips with trembling fingers, I took a tiny sip. Then another. I'd been starving when I got home, but now my appetite had vanished.

Taking my wine into the living room, I flipped on my TV and settled in on the couch.

Cannon hadn't even asked me about rent. If he thought he was staying here for free, simply because he was my best friend's brother, he was dead wrong. I should at least be compensated for the inconvenience of having to share my space.

Several more sips of wine and my muscles began to relax. Enchilada hopped up beside me and nuzzled against my arm. I picked him up and set all six pounds of him on my lap.

"Sorry, buddy. Looks like you're not going to be the man of the house anymore," I murmured, petting his feather-soft fur. While that statement was true, I had no idea how complicated my life was about to become.

Chapter Five

Cannon

At the mall, I'd stocked up on socks, underwear, jeans, and some long-sleeved pullovers. I grabbed a second pair of shoes too. When my place was ransacked I'd been at class, which meant my only surviving possessions had been the clothes on my back, plus my backpack and laptop. Friends had loaned me things, and although the insurance check hadn't come in yet, it was time to restock with essentials.

I went to a mega-center, one of those places open twenty-four hours, and I'd gotten pillows, sheets, towels, shampoo, bodywash, a couple of disposable razors, and a new electric toothbrush. As I walked by a display of fresh flowers, an idea struck me. I picked up a big bouquet of wildflowers, then headed off to find the pet aisle. Tossing a package of dog treats in my cart, I grinned wryly. Maybe this was all part of being a good roommate. Then again, maybe I wanted to fuck her more than I wanted to admit to myself. Shaking the thoughts away, I headed off to the check-out.

I wasn't used to women turning down my advances, but even I knew that Paige's reluctance to fall into bed with me was actually a good thing. I'd gotten myself into a fuck-ton of trouble over women in the past, and if there was one thing my life needed, it was less complications. Paige was tempting and gorgeous, but I was a strong enough man to abide by the "look, but don't touch" rule. Between clinical rotations and preparing for my board exams, the last thing I needed was things becoming weird between me and my new roommate. And while a vow of total celibacy had been a stupid idea, the least I could do was stick by my new rules—one night only, no names or numbers. And that definitely included not fucking my new roomie.

It was just before ten when I arrived back at Paige's place. True to her word, the door was left unlocked, and once I got all my shopping bags inside, I locked us in for the night. After carrying everything down the hall, I stood at the entrance to the guest room that would be my temporary home for the next two months. The door to Paige's bedroom was closed, and while I didn't know for sure if she was sleeping or not, I knew she was tucked in for the night.

Grabbing my shampoo and bodywash from the plastic bag, I headed across the hall for a much-needed shower. Being elbow-deep in vagina all day necessitated that, not that I minded too much. Although it wasn't a field I wanted to pursue, even I had to admit it was a pretty cool experience getting to deliver babies.

I turned on the water and stripped down while waiting for it to heat up. But when I stepped into the shower, I was hit with the mouthwatering scent of Paige's floral shampoo and bodywash. *God damn* . . . My cock instantly leaped to attention. I couldn't resist reaching down to grip my already rock-hard erection.

Squirting some of Paige's conditioner into my palm, I let her scent surround me as I pumped up and down in uneven pulls, the slick cream letting my fist glide over the steely flesh, each stroke bringing a wave of pleasure.

Standing under the hot spray, I thought of Paige and her luscious tits and pink cheeks as she drank in the first sight of me in five years. I wanted to do wicked things to her. Wanted to see if she'd squeak in surprise when my tongue lapped between her thighs. To find out how fast I could make her come. Would I have to work at it, learning how to pleasure her by following the sounds she made, or would she explode quickly? She did seem pretty pent up . . .

I gritted my teeth as my orgasm surged closer. Fuck, I was already about to blow. Normally I'd last much longer, but everything about this woman went straight to my cock. Moments later, my release crashed through me as I emptied into my hand, spent and breathing hard.

After rinsing off a final time, I shut off the water. With water sluicing down my body, I reached for my towel and realize I'd forgotten one. *Fuck.* I'd left my new towels still folded in the shopping bag. Across the hall in my room. Didn't matter. I was ninety-nine percent sure Paige was asleep in her bedroom. Grabbing my dirty clothes from the floor, I opened the bathroom door, moving with purpose toward my room—

When I ran *bang* into something solid. The impact knocked the pile of clothes I'd been holding in front of my groin out of my hands.

A gray-and-brown blur flashed by my feet with a

jingle of tags. Paige gasped in surprise and stumbled a step back. Instinctively, I reached out to steady her, gripping her shoulders.

"I'm sorry," I murmured, noticing that she slept in nothing but a T-shirt that barely covered her ass. The thin material hugged her curves and left her delicious rack on display.

After she righted herself, Paige's gaze wandered down the length of my nude torso, stopping at my crotch. Her eyes widened and her full lips parted, the apples of her cheeks turning a pretty shade of pink. My erection hadn't fully died yet; my spent cock still hung long and heavy between my thighs. And under her heated gaze, it twitched with interest, thickening and beginning to rise again.

"You can touch it if you want," I murmured, amused by her response. There had been more than just astonishment in those wide, pretty eyes. I was pretty sure there was interest, and maybe even desire.

A noise of strangled surprise escaped her lips.

This was just too much fun. I wasn't in a hurry to

go anywhere, but I cleared my throat and her gaze jumped back up to mine.

"You okay?" I asked.

"Enchilada had to pee," she murmured, breathless.

Right, the dog. So *that* was what had run past us into Paige's bedroom. I nodded once, a smirk pulling up my mouth. I'd have to sneak the little mop a few thank-you treats in the morning. This was the most fun I'd had all day.

"Good night," she squeaked, then darted around me into her bedroom, where she promptly slammed the door. I could imagine her behind it, her legs sagging as she braced herself on the wall, her chest heaving as she tried to recover.

Pulling a deep breath into my own lungs, I retrieved my clothes from the floor, chuckling. Then I headed to my room. Dressed in a pair of boxer briefs, I worked on making my bed and firmly telling my dick to calm down. Paige might be gorgeous and tempting— and based on her reaction to the sight of me naked, long overdue for a good shafting—but it didn't matter. I wouldn't be going there. As sweet as that honey might be, I would *not* be having a taste.

I set my alarm for five a.m. and tried like hell to relax so I could get some sleep. Soon I'd be starting a four-week rotation for cardiology, and knew I'd need all my focus. But even though I was exhausted, I was still wound too tight for sleep to come easily. I heaved an annoyed sigh. Sure would be nice to blow off some steam with a tumble between the sheets . . .

God dammit, no. Don't even think about it. That just wasn't in the cards for Paige and me.

I'd have to be more careful. Feeling her hungry gaze on my cock wasn't something I'd be able to resist if I slipped up again.

Chapter Six

Paige

"Paige, your ten-thirty interview is here," my assistant Tabitha called into my office.

"Be right there." I rose from my desk and grabbed the résumé and interview guide for the office-manager candidate I hoped was a good match. As human resources manager for a small nonprofit company, our lack of an actual office manager meant that the extra workload fell on me. I was more than ready to get someone hired into the position. Saying a silent prayer that this person would work out, I made my way to the conference room where Ben Stevens was waiting.

"Good morning." I greeted him, reaching out to shake his hand. He looked a little young, but age didn't matter. As long as he had the qualifications and the professionalism to back it up, we'd be good.

As I sat down and began the interview, my mind wandered to Cannon. He'd been gone this morning by the time I got up. For a moment, I thought I'd dreamed everything that had happened yesterday afternoon. But the evidence of his early-morning rituals had been there: a damp towel hanging next to mine in the bathroom, a coffee mug in the sink. But even more intriguing had been a large bouquet of fuchsia and crimson wildflowers that had been sitting in a glass of water on my kitchen table, along with a package of dog biscuits. It was a nice gesture; I'd give him that.

Only once I was in the shower had the memory of our late-night encounter come rushing back. My eyes had shot open, soap bubbles stinging as I blinked and gasped under the harsh spray. There was no forgetting last night.

Now *that* wouldn't have seemed out of place in a dream—one I'd deny in the morning and replay with my BOB at night. His nude body rivaled those marble sculptures at the art museum. I'd been overwhelmed at the sheer size and hard maleness of him. Broad shoulders, toned pecs leading down to six fully defined abs, and a tapered waist, the likes of which I'd only seen on male models. The fine smattering of hair told me he manscaped thoroughly and often. And the way he'd stood there, still damp and flushed from the shower, his smirk unapologetic, his large half-erect penis hanging between his legs like an anaconda escaped from the zoo . . . a warm shudder passed through me at the memory.

"Uh . . . ma'am? Is something wrong?" Ben asked, breaking off his response to the question I'd posed thirty seconds ago and now couldn't remember.

Shit. I nodded rapidly. "I'm fine, thank you. Just a little tired. Please continue."

I was the exact opposite of fine. Every detail of Cannon's naked body refused to leave my head—and that stuff just wasn't something I should know about my best friend's little brother. But it was too late. My brain was permanently altered. From here on out, I wouldn't be able to think of him as anything other than a sexual being.

And the thing that had really gotten to me?

Cannon's voice had remained calm and certain, like he wasn't the least bit embarrassed about standing on display before me. He'd remained rooted there, shamelessly confident, letting me peruse him in all his glory. And he watched me watch him, his eyebrow raised flirtatiously, almost as though he was challenging me to react. Daring me to look my fill, come closer, touch him, satisfy my . . . curiosity.

Clearing my throat, I picked up Ben Stevens's résumé. "Can you go into more detail about your previous role, and how that fit into your planned career path?" Hopefully I could get my shit together enough to pay attention and evaluate his experience this time.

Ben dutifully launched into a dull and lengthy description of every task required of him at his old company. I jotted notes as he spoke, trying to focus on him and not my body's breathless, heart-pounding reaction to the memory of Cannon.

Twenty minutes later, I still didn't have any idea if Ben was the right person for the job. My brain was so scrambled, I was having a hard time concentrating.

"Can you tell me why you're interested in the office-manager role?" I asked.

Ben's brows drew together and he frowned. "You already asked me that."

"Right." I nodded, smiling while screaming

internally.

My phone vibrated on the conference table beside me. I grabbed it, grateful for the brief reprieve—until I saw it was a text from Cannon. Flipping the phone over on the table without reading it, I took a deep breath. I didn't want to be rude to my candidate. But knowing there was a text waiting for me from Cannon meant I was even less focused on what Ben was saying than before.

A few minutes later I ended the interview, thanking him for his time, and told him I'd be in touch. Once he was headed toward the lobby where the receptionist would show him out, I lunged for my phone, typing my passcode wrong twice before finally getting it right.

CANNON: *Sorry about last night. I hope you weren't too traumatized.*

My jaw dropped open. God, the man was ballsy. I'd give him that. Most people would want to forget the whole thing ever happened. Yet here he was, calling attention to it, trying to push me for a response. Or maybe he was just trying to embarrass me.

Well, fuck that. If he wanted me to freak out—or collapse onto his dick in surrender—he was messing with the wrong girl.

PAIGE: *Next time you want me to see you naked, ask first.*

CANNON: *Noted.*

I chuckled to myself before realizing that I'd implied there was going to be a *next time*. My laughter died on my lips. I'd unintentionally given him the upper hand.

CANNON: *I have a rare weekend off, so I just wanted to check in and see if you had any weekend plans. Don't want to cramp your style.*

PAIGE: *No plans as of yet.*

I hoped I didn't sound too lame typing that.

CANNON: Then I guess I'll see you at home.

I tucked my phone into the pocket of my jeans, trying to ignore the warning bells ringing in my head. I headed back to my office at the far end of the building, my heart thrumming with the news that I'd be subjected to forty-eight hours of Cannon's sexiness.

On one hand, I couldn't deny I was looking forward to the eye candy. And it would be refreshing to have a conversation partner who responded with words instead of barks and tail wags. But I liked my routine; I was used to a certain amount of alone time. If Cannon was this distracting when he wasn't even physically present, how could I hope to be around him all weekend without losing my mind?

"Well, how was he?" Tabitha asked from her perch at the desk outside my office.

"Who?" I asked, irrationally fearful that I'd

somehow let it slip about my new roommate.

"The candidate, Ben," she said.

"Oh, right." I nodded. "He was . . . okay."

She narrowed her eyes. "Are you feeling all right? You look a little flushed."

I cleared my throat. "Fine. I have an early lunch today with a friend. I'll see you later." I discarded Ben's résumé and interview folder on my desk, grabbed my purse, and hightailed it from the office.

Once Allie and I were seated at our favorite casual soup-and-salad restaurant, she grinned at me like she was in on a secret I wasn't.

"Well . . ." she prompted, raising her brows. "How did your first night with your new roomie go?" Allie giggled, smiling as she watched me.

Did he tell her about our late-night run-in? The one in which he was butt-naked? My underarms began to sweat. I faked a breezy smile as my brain screamed at me to lie. So I did.

"Uneventful."

"Good, so it should work out fine between you two."

"Mm-hmm."

"That's a relief. I know Cannon's a grown man, but I still worry about him, you know? He's worked so hard to get where he is, and after everything he's been through, he deserves a break."

I nodded. "Uh-huh." Seemingly unable to string together more than two incoherent syllables, I grabbed my menu and started reading over the lunch specials.

"James bid on tickets to a charity gala this weekend. You think you and Cannon would like to go?"

"Me and Cannon?" I almost squeaked. What did *that* mean? Like, as a date? Did she think there was something between us?

"Sure, why not? The three of us should do something fun—get the dream team back together, y'know? Now that he's transferred here to Michigan, I feel like I need to make up for some lost time with him."

Oh, she meant going as a group. I felt both relieved and very stupid. *Get a grip, Paige . . .* Then my brain caught up with the rest of what she'd said.

"Wait, just us three? What about James?" I asked. Wasn't he the one who'd won the tickets in the first place?

She shook her head, frowning. "He's got to work this weekend."

Her fiancé was a real estate agent and spent a lot of evenings and weekends working. It was fine by me, because it meant Allie and I got to spend a lot of girl time together.

"Sure, I'm free." I returned to reading my menu, but inwardly, I was still freaking out. Would Allie suspect my attraction for her brother? Would she be able to read it all over my face as soon as I looked at Cannon? For that matter, might *Cannon* give the game away? He hadn't exactly been subtle about wanting to fuck me . . .

The waiter came by and we ordered, and then it took me a moment to realize Allie was speaking to me.

"Have you signed up yet?" she asked.

"For?" I chewed on my lip, wondering exactly how much of this conversation I'd missed while having dirty thoughts about her brother. *I'm a terrible friend.*

"The new dating app I told you about."

I groaned. That app wasn't for dating so much as no-strings-attached hookups. But I didn't think Allie had gotten that memo along with the rest of America. Before she'd met James, Allie had found some success with it, going out with four different guys in as many weeks—and spilling all the juicy details about each encounter. Even though she was in a serious relationship now, that didn't stop her from wanting to live vicariously through me.

"I know you ultimately want to find true love one day . . . we all do. But this is just practice. While you're waiting for Mr. Right, that doesn't mean you can't enjoy some hot sex."

"I don't know, Allie. I'm not really comfortable with the idea of banging a perfect stranger."

"He wouldn't be a stranger. You'd e-mail, text, and

chat first. Nothing would happen until you were comfortable."

I fiddled with my napkin while I felt Allie's gaze on me. My last relationship had ended over a year ago, and I hadn't been with anyone since my ex. I knew she was trying to help me—and God knew how badly I craved sex sometimes—but it was still irritating to feel like the subject of an emergency intervention.

Did she think all my problems would go away if I jumped on some magical healing cock? A one-night stand wouldn't be helpful or even fun for me; I just wasn't wired like that. I'd be a nervous wreck, convinced I was going to end up on the evening news because my date was a serial killer, or worse, that he'd see the dimples in my butt and freak out.

She leaned in closer and placed her hand over mine. "It's just to get you back on the horse. I worry about you sometimes, Paigey. All you do is work these days."

I went to the gym sometimes too, but I doubted that was going to get her off my back. "I'll think about it," I said as two massive salads were delivered to our table. Seriously, who could eat this much salad?

I felt my to-do list growing. Not only did I need to resist Cannon's charms, but I needed to find a way to keep Allie off my back about dating, go to a charity gala with her and my new secret crush without her discovering anything, and choose a new office manager at work. My stomach tightened, and I pushed the uneaten salad around on my plate.

My lunch with Allie was supposed to calm me, but I felt more anxious than ever.

Chapter Seven

Cannon

"Found a place to live yet?" Peter asked.

Peter was a nurse anesthetist at the hospital I work at. He was a few years older than me, and in some ways, he treated me like a little brother. We met my first week at the hospital and just clicked. When he got married to his boyfriend of a decade last year, I was one of the groomsmen. And when I needed a place to crash after getting evicted from my apartment this week, he offered to let me crash at this place. But I knew that wasn't a long-term solution. I didn't want to impose on the newlyweds.

I nodded. "I've been staying with my sister's friend Paige." *My sister's very hot friend who I wanted to nail.* I was pretty sure I'd been walking around all day half hard. Guess it was a good thing he hadn't noticed.

"Gotcha." He nodded. "How's that going?"

"It's good. It's just taking some adjustment. I just

moved in yesterday, and I've lived alone for a while, you know?" And now I had to deal with the soft feminine scent of her shampoo in the bathroom, and watching her parade around in yoga pants and talk in gibberish to her dog. She was maddeningly hot and she didn't even know it.

"I still don't understand," Peter said, bending down to tie his bright purple tennis shoe. "How could they just kick you out of your place?"

He was right. My rent check was always on time, and I was quiet and neat. But the personal drama that tagged along with me was apparently more than my landlord wanted to handle. I shrugged. Having your place vandalized four times in six months and broken into twice was a bit excessive.

"Doesn't matter," I muttered. I actually liked being near Paige. Maybe too much.

"So, tell me about your new roomie. Do we like her?" Peter grinned.

"Fuck off," I muttered, stalking away from Peter and his laughter echoing in the halls of the hospital.

● ● ●

True to her word, Paige returned home from work a few minutes after five.

"In here," I called from the kitchen. Enchilada hovered around my feet, poised to snatch any fallen scraps.

She set down a laptop bag on the dining table, her gaze reluctantly dragging over to mine. "Hi."

Wondering if she was remembering how I looked naked, I fought off a smile. "How was work?" I tossed a handful of sliced peppers into a wok, then added some onion.

"Fine," she said, moving a couple of steps closer. "What's all this?"

Enchilada wandered over, the desire to greet his master momentarily winning out over hunger, and Paige reached down to pat his fluffy head.

"I grabbed the ingredients for fajitas at the store today."

"Oh." She looked down at the chicken strips

already browning in the skillet.

"Hope that's okay. You named your dog Enchilada, so I assumed you like Mexican food."

"Of course. It's just . . . I didn't expect you to cook for me."

I shrugged. "I have my first couple of days off in what seems like forever. And besides, I had a craving. Would you mind stirring that chicken?"

She took a rubber spatula from the crock that held her utensils on the counter and turned over each piece of chicken, concentrating on her task carefully.

"I got tequila, and margarita mix too," I said.

She eyed me carefully, her expression serious, but still somehow playful. "Tequila? Do you really think that's a good idea for us?"

I laughed at her honesty. "Hey, we survived night one, didn't we?"

"Yes, and it was a small miracle since you were naked."

I smirked. "Sorry about that. It was an honest mistake."

Paige moved on, busying herself filling the blender with ice, and I couldn't help but notice the pink tinge to her cheeks.

While she mixed the drinks, I sautéed the vegetables and combined them with the chicken. The whir of the blender drowned out the silence around us, and then Paige poured two margaritas into festive glasses.

"Thank you for the flowers, by the way. And the treats for Enchilada. That was thoughtful of you."

I nodded. "It was nothing. I'm just happy to have a place to stay."

I wouldn't tell Paige, but I'd been a little traumatized after staying with Peter and his husband. I was fine with whatever happened in their bedroom, but drew the line at being forced to overhear it. No one should hear their friend shouting for his husband to take him deeper.

"We never got to discuss rent. How much would

you like me to pay?" I asked.

"I . . . I'm not sure." Paige's teeth sank into her lower lip.

Damn, that was distracting. "I'll pay half of the rent and utilities. Just let me know how much it is."

"Okay." She nodded. "I suppose that's fair. Your half will be seven hundred, and it's due on the first of the month. I'll let you know about the utilities."

"Perfect."

I turned off the burners and grabbed a couple of plates. "Do you need to change before dinner? I've got this."

Shaking her head, she took a sip of her frosty drink. "That's okay. Fridays are casual dress."

I recalled that yesterday, she'd been wearing a skirt and a silk blouse. Today she looked just as tempting in a pair of dark jeans that hugged her curves, and a fitted, long-sleeved burgundy T-shirt. A long gold necklace hung around her neck, a sparkly pendant swaying as she moved.

After making up our plates, we carried them into the dining half of the main room. Luckily, the empty silence was soon filled with Paige's questions about med school, a topic I could talk about for hours.

"Do you have classes during the day, and then internships at night? That seems like an awful lot." She looked down at her plate. "Sorry, I don't know how this stuff works."

I waved her off. "Not at all. I finished my classroom time during my first two years. The next two years of med school are spent in rotations. Basically, I'm like a doctor without the medical license. I've delivered babies, assisted with surgery, tended to gunshot victims in the ER. It's a little bit of everything."

"Wow. That sounds intense."

I shrugged. "My stepdad once said you're not a real doctor unless you can handle traumas. Kind of a weird statement, but something about it resonated with me. I'm glad I got to experience that firsthand in my emergency-medicine rotation. Basically, if you're ever stabbed or have a flesh-eating virus, I'm your man."

She laughed as she took another bite of her fajita. Salsa landed on her cheek, and she quickly wiped it away.

"It's smart the way they structure it," I said, "because you're forced to learn everything before you can declare your specialty. And then after that, you apply for residencies."

"Right . . . your residency. Allie said you'd be moving in about two months."

I nodded. "That's the idea." I just had to figure out where in the hell I wanted to go. Part of me wanted to whisk off on an adventure, maybe go and live overseas, do humanitarian aid in India or Africa for a few years. But I knew Mom and Allie would freak if I did that, so I was torn.

"So you liked working with trauma patients? Is that what you want to specialize in?" Paige placed her napkin back in her lap and looked at me expectantly.

I let out a deep sigh. "Honestly? I don't have a fucking clue. Emergency medicine is what I've been telling everyone for the past two years, but the truth is, I don't know. I deferred the decision, and the final deadline is approaching in a couple of weeks. I need to just pick something, but so far I haven't been able to narrow it down."

"Ah, I see." She rubbed her chin. "You're a fear-of-commitment type."

At that, I chuckled. She didn't even know the half of it. "Something like that."

"What's your current rotation? Do you like it?"

Oh, this was going to be fun. I couldn't wait to see the blush on her cheeks when I told her. "Obstetrics and gynecology. And yeah, it's been . . . enlightening. But if I'm going to have my hand inside a woman's honeypot, I'd much rather it be for pleasure than for work."

She choked on her margarita, coughing to clear her airway. "Fuck." Coughing loudly several more times into her napkin, she grinned at me. "That was not fair."

I merely shrugged. "Never said I played fair, princess."

"You shouldn't piss off the woman who so graciously offered you a roof over your head. I'll tell Allie you've been making trouble." Paige waved her fork at me. The menace was spoiled by the tiny smile that tugged at the corner of her mouth. "So you only enjoy vaginas recreationally. Got it. What rotations *did* you like? Any favorites?"

I chewed slowly as I pondered. "Hmm . . . maybe cardiology?"

"What appeals to you about it?"

"I don't know."

I did know, but it would sound stupid if I explained it out loud. After Dad left, Mom was so sad and crying all the time. When I'd asked her what was wrong, she told me that her heart was broken . . . and it scared the shit out of me. I'd been too young to understand that the literal, physical heart wasn't the same thing as what people meant when they talked about emotions. So I'd thought she was going to die.

It made sense to me that the heart pumped emotions along with blood. I, too, had felt things in my chest—a painful squeeze whenever I thought about Dad, a solid warmth when I resolved to protect Mom and Allie no matter what. But even after I learned otherwise, I remained fascinated with the heart, both its symbolism and its reality. It was the only organ in the body that never tired or took a break. Steady and faithful. Ironic, given that I seemed to be cursed when it came to relationships, that I was more interested in matters of the heart than the physiology of it.

After a few more bites of her food, Paige looked up. "Why did you decide to go into medicine?"

I rubbed the back of my neck. "You already know my sister and I were dealt a crap hand."

She looked down into her margarita. "Yeah, I do . . . I was there. It wasn't always easy."

Being raised by a single mom with only a high-school education wasn't glamorous. We moved more times I cared to remember. It seemed like every time my mom lost her job or broke up with her latest boyfriend, we were uprooted. She made sure we stayed in the same school district, but finding a place with rent she could afford wasn't easy. Without a father figure in our lives, the responsibility of being the man of the house fell on me.

"Growing up the way I did, I guess it shaped my goals. Now I'm just perfecting the art of making lemonade."

She smiled at me as if she liked that answer. "Making lemonade. I like that. So, what are your goals?"

"Being low-income meant I qualified for free tutoring and a bunch of scholarships. I won plenty of those, based on both merit and need, enough to cover the cost of my tuition at Yale. And then later, med school."

"So you turned a bad situation into a good one."

"I certainly tried like hell to."

I was lucky in some regards. Most of my peers would graduate with student-loan debt up to their eyeballs. Working harder than everyone else had landed me scholarships that probably saved my ass.

"But that still doesn't tell me why medicine." Paige placed her elbows on the table, leaning closer.

"I knew from an early age that one day I'd be taking care of my mom. It was the only thing I was sure of. She'd sacrificed so much for us, did the best she could. Since before I can remember, I've felt like, as her only son, I have a responsibility. I guess subconsciously I chose a field where taking care of others was the focus."

Smiling at me fondly, Paige twirled a piece of her shiny blond hair between her fingers. "You were always such a good kid, a serious student."

"Don't patronize me. I was a nerd." I set my napkin beside my now empty plate.

She laughed, and I couldn't help but smile. "I didn't say that."

"That's only because you were trying to be nice."

She shrugged. "It's rare to be so disciplined about studying and goal-setting at such a young age. You're actually kind of amazing, Cannon. And now you're going to be a doctor in a few short months."

Her compliment radiated through me. I rarely took the time to examine my way of life. I just did the work that was in front of me and kept going.

Of course, things had changed in the past handful of years. My mom had remarried and now my stepdad provided for her, so she technically didn't need me to support her anymore. But she was immensely proud of what I'd accomplished, so I just continued on making lemonade, living the only way I knew how.

We finished dinner and carried our dishes to the kitchen. Standing side by side, she rinsed while I loaded the dishwasher. We made a pretty good team. Our new living arrangement should have felt strange, with all our old history and this new sexual tension crackling between us, yet it felt natural in a way I didn't anticipate.

"Any big plans for tonight?" Paige asked, handing me the last dish.

I shook my head. "Not really. I may go out with some friends later, grab a beer. You're welcome to come along." I wondered what she'd make of Peter and his husband, Azan.

"No, that's okay. I brought my laptop home. There's a couple of work things I need to get done."

"Work on a Friday night?"

I made a low sound of disapproval in my throat, but the truth was, her presence would cramp my plans if I was going to pick someone up. And something told me that alcohol plus Paige was a bad combination. All of our inhibitions would be lowered. Not that I was going to fall into bed with her—I had enough self-control to prevent that. Well, probably. But who knew what I might say? I couldn't go admitting that the fifteen-year-old me used to jack off to her yearbook photo every night. I'd have my man card revoked.

"Did Allie mention that charity event to you tomorrow?" she asked, chewing on her lower lip.

I wiped my hands on a dishtowel. "I told her I'd go. You?"

She nodded. "I guess I'll see you tomorrow, then. Have fun tonight." She grabbed her laptop bag from the floor of the dining room and disappeared to her room, like she was desperate to get away from me.

But what had I expected? We'd drink tequila and reminiscence about the past? Actually, yeah, I'd been kind of hoping we would. I guessed there was always tomorrow.

After a nice dinner together and easy conversation, I was pleased to see that perhaps our new living arrangement would work. Yes, I was sexually attracted to her, but that didn't mean I'd ever act on it.

I headed to my room since I still had an hour before I was to meet up with the other interns from my program and a few friends from the hospital. Collapsing onto my horribly uncomfortable futon bed, I stuffed a pillow under my head and let out a heavy sigh.

Paige had been a surprise tonight. She was down to earth and easy to talk to. Optimistic and sweet. I knew I was cramping her style being here, but she handled it all with such grace. Of course, I wished she hadn't felt the need to sneak off to her bedroom under the guise of having to work, but whatever. Everyone needed alone time occasionally. I was the same way. After a busy shift at the hospital, I craved silence.

Fishing my phone from my jeans pocket, I opened a social media app I seldom used. For some reason, I found myself typing Paige's name into the search bar, clicking ENTER, and then waiting while it pulled up her photo.

I clicked through the few photos she had shared, noting that most of them were either selfies or pictures of her and my sister. There didn't seem to be a boyfriend in any of the shots, which was odd. She was gorgeous, and most of all *normal*. I didn't know why I couldn't seem to attract a nice, normal girl.

After tossing the phone onto the mattress beside me, I pressed the heels of my hands against my eyes and took a deep breath. Just looking at her had my cock rising. Knowing she was in the next room and there wasn't a damn thing I could do about my attraction to her was a bitch of a combination. I wasn't used to having to exercise such self-control.

My hand wandered under my jeans, adjusting where my now hard cock was pressing into the zipper. Biting down on my lip, I took the weight of my cock in my hand and began to stroke.

I told myself it was merely cleaning out the pipes before I went out for the evening. It's not like I could bring a girl home to Paige's place.

Unbuttoning my jeans, I freed myself from the denim prison. Stroking in hard pulls, I imagined how Paige's small, soft hand would feel moving up and down my shaft, her delicate fingers massaging my balls. With a swallowed grunt of pleasure, I pumped faster, racing toward my release.

A noise of surprise caught my attention, and I opened my eyes to see Paige standing in my doorway.

Fuck!

Unable to tuck my swollen cock back into my jeans, I pulled a pillow into my lap and gazed up at her. "Are you here to lend a hand, princess?"

Her face turned tomato red and she stammered out an apology before scurrying off down the hall.

After a few deep breaths to get myself under control, I tucked a very unhappy camper back into my pants and went in search of her. Paige was in the living room, standing in front of the window, her shoulders tense.

When she heard me approach, she turned to face me. "Oh my God, I am so sorry." Her expression was pained, and I could tell she genuinely felt terrible. "I didn't mean to just barge in like that."

"Then why did you?"

"I thought I heard you say my name."

Fuck. Had I? I blew out a frustrated breath and pushed my hands into my hair.

Paige crossed the room and sat on the edge of the couch. "I'm sorry, but I don't think this is going to work."

Still reeling and on edge, I took another deep breath. Lacing my fingers behind my neck, I stood before her. Her cheeks were still stained pink, and her eyes were glassy.

"I get it. You don't think we can stay together under one roof without fucking each other's brains out."

She made a noise of surprise in her throat. "I didn't say that."

"You didn't have to, princess. Your reactions to me told me everything I needed to know."

Paige's blue eyes widened, locking onto mine. I'd given her one hell of a shock. But the look in her eyes was far from disgusted or angry.

Fuck. Playing with her was almost too easy. And fun.

Aside from her physical response to me, I knew she was recalling the first time I'd called her princess all those years ago. I was a rotten ten-year-old, and she and Allie were entering their freshman year of high school. Things had changed between us. I was no longer their cute little sidekick. I was a disease they couldn't seem to shake. They didn't want me near them, and since I was too young to understand it, let alone communicate my feelings about it, I'd lashed out.

Paige was the furthest thing from a spoiled princess. She was kind, considerate, and humble. But her family was solidly middle class, and ours was . . . well, not. It was a nickname meant to sting when I hurled it at her. Only it hadn't stung at all. She'd smirked at me, her mouth lifting in a crooked smile, and ruffled her fingers through my hair. After that, I continued using it because the nickname often earned me a smile.

"You can't tell me you're not interested. The way your tight little nipples poke out, begging to be licked, the hammering of your pulse in your throat, the flush of your cheeks, the greedy way your eyes fell to my lap when you walked in."

She chewed on her lower lip, her gaze darting away from mine.

"It's nothing to be ashamed of. We have chemistry. Plain and simple," I continued, my tone soft, alluring.

"I do not . . ." She anchored her hands to her hips, which pressed her breasts out, her beaded nipples still hard and straining.

I suppressed a laugh. She could deny it all she wanted, but I was a fourth-year med student. I'd been studying biology and anatomy for years. She had all the classic signs. She was turned on.

"We're practically family, Cannon. Allie would—"

"We're *not* family. But yeah, Allie would freak the fuck out, which is why we'd never tell her."

"It's not going to happen. Ever." Her voice wavered. It was slight, but it was there.

I shrugged. "Whatever you say. It was just an idea." And obviously a bad one.

Part of me was relieved she refused my suggestion. If I broke Paige's heart, not only would my sister kick my ass, but I wouldn't forgive myself. But toying with her like this, watching her reactions to me . . . that I couldn't resist.

Pulling a deep breath into her lungs, Paige fought to regain control.

"Listen, if you don't want me here, if you don't think we can *behave* . . ." I lifted my brows suggestively. "I can find somewhere else to crash until the end of the semester."

After a scoffed grunt, she straightened her spine. "I can behave like an adult if you can. It's only two months."

So she admits that mis*behaving appeals to her.* "Sounds reasonable," I murmured.

Actually it sounded fucking depressing, but I wouldn't push her. If she wanted to deny she was interested, there wasn't much I could do. And given my track record with women, it was a damn good idea to keep it in my pants.

My career was the one thing in my control. It felt good to set goals and work toward them. Growing up, we moved from one run-down apartment to the next until Mom remarried when I was eighteen, and she moved in with my stepdad when I went off to college. Things stabilized after that, but by then the desire for more was ingrained in me so deeply that nothing could stop me now. I wanted to do better, to prove to my mom that I could make something of myself.

Yes, the need for pussy often forced me into clubs seeking a quick release with a willing partner. One-night stands and the occasional short-term relationship helped squelch the burning need low in my groin. But it never detracted from my mission. And after this last particularly painful breakup, I was done with relationships, even short-term ones. From here on out, I would stick to clinical matters of the heart, and avoid the metaphorical ones that often landed you in a messy breakup.

"I really didn't mean to interrupt," Paige said, her voice softening. "Are you mad?"

I shook my head and sat down beside her. "I'm not mad. Horny? Yes. Mad, no."

She gave me a sweet smile, her blue eyes crinkling in the corners. There was no way I could be mad at her. I just needed to figure out how to survive the next two months.

Chapter Eight

Paige

Cannon got home just after midnight. I hated myself that I'd waited up, listening for him, but I had. He came home alone, used the bathroom—I'd heard his electric toothbrush humming through the thin wall, the water running—and then closed the door to his bedroom.

Our encounter earlier that evening had played through my mind for hours. It was twice now I'd seen him naked, and I knew I'd never erase the images from my brain. I couldn't believe the man he'd grown into. And that foul mouth on him?

Your tight little nipples are poked out, begging to be licked . . .

Remembering the way his darkly seductive voice rolled over the words sent a fresh wake of goose bumps skittering down my spine.

Thankfully, the morning passed by quickly. Cannon

went to the gym and showered while I headed out for a hair appointment to touch up my color and cut before the charity gala. It worked out perfectly that my regularly scheduled appointment fell on the day of the event. I left the salon feeling refreshed and optimistic. At least my blowout wouldn't go to waste.

Allie promised she'd be by at four to pick us up for the event. When I arrived home, I touched up my makeup and picked out a dress to wear. I slipped into a champagne-colored cocktail dress with a high neckline and plunging back that I'd picked up last year at a designer sample sale but never had an excuse to wear. The cut of the dress didn't allow for a bra, but it was so well fitted that I didn't think anyone would notice. My long hair was blown out in soft waves that tumbled down my back.

I could hear Cannon moving around in the house, and for some strange reason, I felt nervous about seeing him.

Slipping my feet into the tall black heels I'd regret within the hour, I was ready. As I added my grandma's beautiful vintage diamond earrings, I checked my appearance in the full-length mirror on the back of my closet door. The high heels elongated my legs, and the dress shimmered in the light.

My mind wandered back to last night. His making dinner for us had been such an unexpectedly sweet gesture, and our conversation had flowed so easily. I'd thought I already knew him pretty well, but there had been more to discover. I'd seen bits of his past as we talked—the way his mouth had tightened and his brows turned down when he spoke of his modest upbringing, the upbringing that had inspired him to strive for more, and the hope in his eyes when he'd told me about practicing medicine. I liked this new, adult version of Cannon.

It was strange. As much as I'd detested the idea of having a roommate at first, I found the company to be pleasantly refreshing. I even felt safer, slept better, with him under the same roof. Maybe it was because we were more alike than I'd remembered. I understood Cannon's philosophy on—*how did he say it? oh, yeah*—the art of making lemonade. I understood it better probably than anyone.

My mother had always told me I was a careful and overly cautious little girl. From the time I could walk, I was serious and often worried. Always the responsible one, someone friends could count on. Then I lost my parents within a year of each other after my high school graduation, and my world became dark and lonely. It took several months before I realized it was up to me to make it better, and I wouldn't tarnish their memory by falling apart.

I'd never done anything wild or reckless or foolish. I took care of people. It was what I did. I guess, in my own way, I was making lemonade. I enjoyed my work as human resources manager for a non-profit, I took in Enchilada off the street when I found him wandering without a collar, Allie and I stuck by each other through thick and thin. I just carried on. One day after another. Of course I wanted more, wanted to find someone to share my life with, but that would happen in time. Though the conversation and meal last night with a man who'd been attentive and sweet only cultivated that feeling inside me more.

Deciding I couldn't procrastinate any longer, I headed out to see if Cannon was ready too. I found him standing in the kitchen, loading a plate and a glass into the dishwasher.

He was bent at the waist, and my eyes zeroed in on his firm ass. *Holy shit.* The man had the body of a Greek god. The air left my lungs as I drank in the view. Yep, it had been entirely too long since I'd gotten laid.

As he rose to face me, a slow smile spread across his lips. I'd been caught. I quickly looked away, but the damage was done.

"Ready?" I asked, breathless.

Cannon looked scrumptious in a black suit, crisp white dress shirt that was fitted enough to hint at the muscle beneath, and a wine-colored tie. His hair was messy and his jaw held a dusting of a shadow. His body was so masculine, so heavy with the promise of sex, that it drew mine like a magnet.

Rather than answer, Cannon's smile faded and his gaze slipped from mine. My body heated under his perusal as his gaze drifted over the swell of my breasts, the curve of my hips. If it was possible to spontaneously combust under the weight of his stare, I was about to find out.

"Get a good look?" I finally managed to say, scolding him.

"Did you?" he asked, his voice much too controlled. "Shall I spin around for you? Maybe get naked again?" He chuckled after that last part, and I felt my face heat.

Yes, unfortunately, I'd already seen what was underneath his clothes—a six-pack of abs, and a large hoo-ha between his legs. Like that was a memory I'd soon forget.

Placing one hand on my hip, I fought for control of my body's reaction to his incredibly masculine one. "Aren't doctors supposed to have more . . ." My lips twitched, looking for the right word.

"Bedside manner?" he offered after a moment.

"Tact," I deadpanned before my brain could fixate too much on the way he said *bed*.

The knock at the door grabbed our attention. Allie was here.

Thank freaking God. I snatched my postage-stamp-sized purse from the counter on my way to the front door.

"Are you guys ready?" Allie asked, looking adorable in a black shift dress.

Cannon stepped into his size 12 black dress shoes and slipped his cell into his pocket. The movement drew my eyes to the front of his dress slacks, and my face heated.

Dammit.

Allie drove since she was the one who invited us. When we arrived, the valet whisked her car away while we climbed the steps to the stunning museum where the event was being held. I'd only been here once, on a class field trip almost two decades ago.

Tail-coated waiters weaved through the crowd, balancing glasses of pink champagne on serving trays, and platters of enticing food lined the long banquet tables on the far side of the room. A seven-piece band played soft jazz, creating a rich, cultured atmosphere. Pretty people mingled and laughed and made small talk.

I recognized the song playing as one by Dean Martin, and smiled as Allie flagged down a nearby waiter, grabbing glasses of bubbly for the three of us.

"How's it going so far, roomies?" Allie smiled, looking between me and her brother.

I swallowed a sudden lump in my throat. "Fine," I lied. I was terrified my face was going to betray my growing attraction for the man who was currently standing way too fucking close to me.

"Paige has been great," Cannon said smoothly. "Very welcoming."

"There's not many people I'd trust to take in my little brother," Allie said.

"You do realize I'm a grown man?" Cannon asked pointedly.

Allie merely shrugged. She'd always been that way with him—an overprotective mother hen. In a way, I felt a little bad for him, although her intentions were good.

"Did you sign up yet?" Allie nudged me with her

elbow and gave me a side-eyed glance.

Not this shit again. I inwardly groaned. If she was so happy with her love life, why did she feel the need to try to orchestrate mine?

"Not yet," I murmured, taking another sip of my drink. My gaze drifted to the stage as I tried to lose myself in the music.

"What are you talking about?" Cannon asked.

"An awesome dating app. I'm trying to get Paige back out in the game."

Cannon stiffened, his narrowed eyes finding mine in an appraising look, as if there was something he didn't like about the idea of me dating.

"I mean, she's gorgeous. Right, Cannon?" Allie asked.

"Stunning," he said, continuing to stare directly into my eyes. That sizzling connection I'd experienced before returned with full force, making the nape of my neck tingle. His attention was too much, and I had to look away.

"Seriously, Paige," Allie continued. "Your days of being a nun are over. I'm not going to stop until you've signed up."

"You've never bugged me about this," Cannon said.

"That's because if you started dating seriously, I'd have something to say about that. You're so close to completing med school, Cannon. You've made it this far; any distractions now would just be stupid. Especially given your track record."

I looked out onto the stage, the blood pumping so loudly in my ears, I could barely hear the music. Maybe coming out with them tonight had been a bad idea.

"I'm going to get some air." Cannon strode away.

Allie heaved out a sigh. "He's been through a lot these past few weeks. It'll blow over. It always does."

I got the sense that something had happened that I wasn't privy to. Something that made Allie even more protective of Cannon than she usually was. The way he'd stormed off made me sympathetic. That, and I didn't want Allie pressuring me about her stupid dating site again. I would welcome any escape route from *that* conversation.

"Did something happen? With Cannon?" I asked.

"What do you mean?"

"He's a twenty-four-year-old man, Al. Surely he can handle dating on top of school and work if he wants to."

Allie's gaze turned from the stage and onto mine, and she chewed on her lip. "I shouldn't say anything, but he's had a string of bad luck. He attracts some real psychos."

I wasn't really sure what to say. Was Allie just blowing it out of proportion? Her belief that no one was good enough for her amazing younger sibling wasn't exactly a secret. But what if she was telling the truth? What was I even supposed to do with that information?

At any rate, I didn't want to stir up shit in the middle of a fancy party. Whether Allie was micromanaging Cannon's life was their own family business; they could argue about it later if they wanted to. So I just said, "Really? That sucks."

Allie looked like she wanted to say something else, then just nodded, her lips pursed.

We sipped our drinks for a few more minutes. Soon Cannon wandered back. The tension in his brow from earlier was gone, and he seemed relaxed and himself again.

With the awkward conversations behind us, I hoped, we listened to the band in silence. Allie swayed to the music while Cannon and I stood stiffly, mere inches apart, trying not to touch.

The setting should have been an almost overwhelming barrage on my senses; it was noisy, crowded, and provided prime people-watching. Yet all I could focus on was one thing—the man standing next to me. Cannon's spicy male scent, the heat radiating between us. The way he seemed to be distracted by my presence as well only made me more aware, more curious about this mysterious thing developing between us.

One thing was certain—Allie could never know about my growing attraction to her brother dearest. I'd just seen how she reacted to any potential distractions from his career. And what was the point, anyway, if he was moving away in two months? I'd just end up sleeping in an empty bed again, but even lonelier this time, because my best friend would be pissed at me.

"Would you like to dance?" Cannon asked, turning toward me and offering his hand.

What the fuck did he think he was doing? I stared at him in disbelief. Did he *want* to blow our cover?

But before I could answer, Allie's hand was on the small of my back, nudging me forward. "Go for it, Paige. You need all the practice you can get with the opposite sex, and it's not like you're going to fall for Cannon!" She laughed, giving me another shove.

Forcing a smile, I placed my hand in Cannon's and let him guide me onto the dance floor, where other couples were swaying to the soft jazz floating around us.

"Thought I'd save you," Cannon said, his voice rich and silky near my ear.

My posture relaxed almost immediately. So *that* was what this was about. "Thank you."

"She means well, you know."

I nodded. That much was true.

While we danced, Cannon hummed along to the words of the Frank Sinatra song, moving and guiding me in sync with the music. I was starting to realize there were so many little things I didn't know about this man.

Holding my hand in his large palm, Cannon gripped my hip with his other hand as he guided me across the dance floor. I glanced over every so often to see if Allie was watching us, but she wasn't. She was chatting with an older man at the bar.

"Why are you still single?" he asked.

I looked up, inhaling the mouthwatering scent of crisp aftershave on his stubbled jaw.

"You've always been sweet and kind. I half figured you'd be married off by now.

I shrugged. "Not married. Not even close." *Just a soon-to-be thirty-year-old woman living with a dog.*

"I see that. But you've grown into quite a beauty, princess. It makes no sense. Are you sure there's not a reason you're single?"

"No reason. I'm waiting for love," I said, surprised at the honesty in my words. "And he seems to be taking his sweet time."

Cannon nodded. "I see."

As one song ended and blended into the other, Cannon continued to hold me, swaying to the music. We talked again about the art of making lemonade, and that's when I decided I wasn't just attracted to his good looks, or masculine appeal. I was attracted to the man inside, the person he'd grown into.

His words struck something inside me. I'd closed myself off to the idea of a relationship, and I couldn't even explain why.

When the song ended, Cannon led us over to the bar, which was great. I found I suddenly needed something stronger than champagne.

Sipping a cranberry-vodka cocktail, I contemplated what I was doing with my life. Maybe Allie and Cannon were right. I needed to put myself out there more. I had a good job that I enjoyed, a nice home, a comfortable life, but I didn't have anything real. Didn't have a loving connection, someone to come home to, unless you counted Enchilada.

It had only recently started to bother me. Maybe it was because Allie was constantly pointing out my single status that it had been pushed to the forefront of my mind.

A little piece of me wondered if my desire for companionship was triggered by the warm, able-bodied male who was now sharing my space . . .

• • •

A couple of hours later, we'd had our fill of the gala. Allie drove us back to my house, talking of her adventures in planning their wedding. It was obvious that Cannon wasn't any more of a fan of James than I was. He rolled his eyes at the mention of a groom's party. That made me smile.

Stopping at the curb, Allie suddenly looked worried in the dim interior of the car. "You two can stay under the same roof and behave like adults, right?"

Cannon's gaze met mine in the rearview mirror.

"What do you think, Paige?" The hint of a smile on his full, sexy lips worked its way under my skin, taking up permanent residence.

"D-don't be silly," I forced out. My voice sounded unnaturally high and breathless.

"I just don't want to turn on the news one day and find out you murdered each other," Allie said.

I let out a shaky breath. She had no idea about my attraction to him—at least, not for the moment.

"Cannon, you should maybe get some earplugs. She snored like crazy when we shared a college dorm," Allie continued. "And Paigey, don't let Cannon leave all the chores for you. Crack the whip on his ass."

"A whip. Now that's an interesting idea." Cannon chuckled, and I resisted the urge to kick the back of his seat.

Satisfied, Allie turned back toward the front. "Good night, guys."

With uncertainty stirring in my veins, I climbed from the car and followed Cannon inside.

It was still early evening, too early to feign being tired and go to bed, so the only thing I could do was accept Cannon's invitation to have a glass of wine.

I excused myself to change, exchanging my fancy dress and heels for yoga pants and a T-shirt. Then I rejoined Cannon in the living room. He'd shrugged off his jacket, which now hung on the back of a dining chair. His white dress shirt was unbuttoned at the throat, and the sleeves had been rolled up on his forearms.

"Tonight was fun, huh?" he asked, stretching out his lanky frame on my small sofa, loosening his tie.

I accepted the glass of wine he offered and sat down in the armchair next to him. Fancy galas weren't generally my thing, but it was nice to change it up once in a while. "I hadn't been to that museum since my sixth-grade field trip. It's so pretty there." The stone building with its massive pillars out front stood like a beautiful reminder of the city's history.

"Allie really wants you to sign up for that dating thing," he said, appraising me. "Are you going to?"

I was sure I was reading more into his sudden interest than was actually there, but the question still triggered a swarm of butterflies inside me. I took another sip of wine to buy myself a few more seconds.

The truth was, I did want to find a good man. And the chances of finding my Mr. Right on a dating app were slim. But maybe that was okay. Maybe a Mr. Fun-for-Now would be nice too. A few decent orgasms wouldn't be the worst thing in the world. I hadn't had sex in well over a year, and according to Allie, that wasn't normal for a woman in her twenties. Maybe I just wasn't as bold and liberated as she was. But why couldn't I be? What was holding me back? Why couldn't I grab life by the balls and live, take my pleasure as I saw fit?

Pushing all that aside, I was much more interested in finding out about Cannon. "I dunno, probably not. What about you? Any interest in dating?"

His expression turned serious, and I wondered if I'd struck a nerve. He couldn't be hung up on Allie's warning, could he? He was a grown man and could date whoever he wanted to.

After a pause he said, "My past has dictated that I live by a strict set of rules when it comes to sex. It only happens once, and no exchanging names or numbers."

I rolled my eyes. "How romantic of you."

"You don't approve?"

"Spoken like a true manwhore."

"It has nothing to do with being a manwhore; I can promise you that. My number is actually fairly low. Healthy, but low."

"What's the point then?" I took another sip of wine, enthralled by his deep, low tone.

"In my experience, women turn into crazed creatures after sex."

I huffed. "Crazed? What the hell is that supposed to mean?" He made it sound as though we were nothing more than delicate hormonal messes who lost their minds at the thought of mating.

"I have a long and storied history with this. Trust me."

"Beginning with?"

"You want to know about my first time?" He grinned and I nodded. Shaking his head, he set his glass down on the table. "I was sixteen when I lost my virginity. Amanda was two grades older, but I'd known her for years."

Was he talking about Amanda McDuff? She'd lived down the street from Allie and Cannon growing up. I could only assume that the blond, blue-eyed cheerleader was who he meant.

"She was nice, normal, friendly. Not a care in the world. I knew she'd fucked Tommy Lester after homecoming the week before. So I casually asked her if she'd like to be my first."

Real smooth. I smirked.

"She said yes and we did the deed."

"And then?"

He looked down at his hands. "She tried to commit suicide two days later."

Jesus. I winced.

"Yeah. And while the situations haven't all been that severe, they've been close. From near strangers who profess their love after a quickie, to stalkers, to one who handcuffed herself to my bed, let's just say I've not been lucky after getting lucky."

"Is your dick cursed with black magic or something?"

He shrugged, dragging his eyes up to meet mine. "No, just eight inches long. I also have wicked stamina . . . and an advanced understanding of female anatomy."

My insides clenched violently. *Fuck.*

Now it was his turn to smirk. "You having a problem there?"

I spread my hands in a *who me?* gesture, my wine sloshing a little in its glass. "Jeez, Cannon. I'm sorry, I'm just a little fucking thrown off here. You're Allie's kid brother."

His smile was devilish. "We're both adults now, Paige. There's no reason we can't discuss sex without it turning weird. Besides, you're the one who brought it up."

I grumbled, but couldn't argue. That much was true. "So, what happened after that?"

"I tried another tactic. For a while last year, I temporarily swore off sex."

"All of it?"

"Well, I'm no saint. Oral was still on the menu. But the actual act of penetration was not."

I made a noise of surprise. Was he serious or just trying to get a rise out of me?

"Turns out women get pretty angry when you refuse to fuck any part of them except their mouths. Even if I offered to return the favor, they took it as a personal insult."

"You think? God, do you hear yourself? You sound like an egomaniacal dick."

He shrugged, a sexy smirk pulling up his lips. "Just protecting my interests."

"Which are?" I knew he was driven, but I didn't know what his precise goals were. Not really, anyway.

"My mom and sister have been through a lot. They've done so much to make sure I get where I am today. I'm *this* close to graduating med school and landing a residency. I won't let pussy, or a woman who thinks we're suddenly in love because I fucked her better than her boyfriend ever could, ruin my future."

The only reply I could manage was "Well said."

During the entire conversation, my heart had been hammering away in my chest. This sexy, forbidden man was giving me a glimpse into his sex life. I could only imagine women throwing themselves at him. Not only was he gorgeous, but he was also a doctor. And if he was telling the truth about how big his cock was . . .

"Why are you looking at me like that?" he asked.

My heart beat fast and loud and hot. "So you really believe that after sleeping with you one time, women fall in love with you?"

He nodded. "I wish it wasn't true, but yeah, that's what I'm telling you."

Something snapped inside me.

Maybe it was the wine, maybe it was the twinkle in his mischievous eyes. Hell, it could have been the eager bulge in his pants, but the fixer in me wanted to help— wanted to prove him wrong. Of course I wanted to experience true love one day, but in the meantime, I was damn near lightheaded at the idea of having a hot tryst.

"What if I could prove you wrong?" My voice was surprisingly steady for how nervous I suddenly felt.

"What are you saying?" His posture was stiff, as if his body was coiled tight, all his muscles on alert.

Wicked thoughts flashed through my brain. I tried like hell to talk myself out of them, but fuck, I'd seen this man naked, and now we were living under the same roof.

"Are you willing to put your money where your mouth is?"

"And have sex with you?" His lips twitched, distracting me.

My eyes met his and held. I didn't even need to say *yes* out loud.

"What's in this for you?" he asked.

"Aside from a few orgasms? The chance to prove your theory is bullshit."

He pushed his hands into his hair and stared up at the ceiling. "Fuck." His voice was thick and laced with need.

Boring Paige had vanished, and in her place, the new Paige was saucy, sexual, and daring. I felt alive and brazen and wicked. I hadn't felt anything like this in the longest time. Besides, we only had to live together for two months. What was the worst that could happen?

"When do we start?" I murmured. The alcohol must have been hitting me much harder than I'd thought, because holy shit, *what?*

He sat forward again. His sin-soaked smile sent the thrill of victory through me. I had won; I was going to get everything I craved. He reached out to stroke his thumb along my cheek, and I couldn't have stopped myself leaning into his touch if I'd wanted to.

"I'm not fucking you when you're drunk." His voice was far too husky to be saying something like that.

"Sleep on it. If you still want to do this tomorrow, I'm game." And then he rose to his feet and disappeared down the hall.

Part of me was pissed off—not to mention so horny I could scream. But most of me was relieved. I unsteadily rose to my feet and headed down the hall for my bedroom. That suggestion had passed "bold" and gone straight into "completely insane."

Cannon had been a gentleman, giving me an out. It was probably for the best. I was sure that by tomorrow morning, I'd come to my senses.

At least, I hoped so.

Chapter Nine

Paige

When I woke up, I was sure last night had just been a bad dream. Then I swung my legs over the side of the bed and saw the champagne-colored cocktail dress crumpled on my floor, frowning as memories of last night clawed at the edges of my brain. But the wet nose of a certain little fluff ball nudged me again. Enchilada had to pee.

I steeled myself and tiptoed into the hall. The house was totally quiet. Cannon's bedroom door was mostly shut, and I rushed past it. I grabbed the leash from the counter, and that's when I saw it.

A Post-it note was stuck to my coffeemaker, Cannon's messy handwritten scrawled across the paper.

We need to talk.

Four little words shouldn't have had the ability to make me break out in hives, but when the reality of last night came crashing back, I had to grip the counter for support. I had actually seriously propositioned Cannon for sex. This was the reality I had to deal with now. Hanging my head in my hands, I inhaled deeply.

If I could stay in my room and hide all day, I would. But then Enchilada let out another whimper.

"Okay. Come on, buddy." I grabbed his leash and slipped my feet into my shoes, and then Enchilada and I were safely outside without making a scene.

I breathed a sigh of relief as we crossed the street to our customary patch of grass . . . and that was when I noticed that Cannon's car was gone. The sinking feeling in my stomach quickly bloomed into full-on panic.

Oh God, had I driven him away with my insane suggestion last night? Maybe he'd gone straight to Allie this morning, told her he was no longer comfortable staying here. I had sexually harassed her baby brother. Holy shit, she was never going to talk to me ever again. I stared at the distant Huron River as Enchilada did his business, and fantasized about throwing myself in.

When Enchilada finished, I gathered him into my arms, holding him tight to my chest as I dashed back inside. The door to Cannon's room had been left ajar, and I nudged it open a few inches further to peek inside. The futon was back into its couch position, and the blankets were folded on top of the desk. His duffel bag and a couple of shopping bags were in the corner. So his stuff was still here, but I wasn't the least bit comforted.

His note was clear and to the point—but what the hell was I going to say to him?

Sure I'd made a colossal mistake last night, I busied myself making coffee and breakfast. Then I took a shower, as if going through the motions of shampooing, shaving, and blow-drying would make everything better.

I couldn't wait for this weekend to be over. I'd never wanted it to be Monday morning so badly before in my entire life. I thought if I could disappear into the office, I could lose myself in my weekly routines and obligations, then everything would go back to normal.

Oh, how wrong I was.

I heard a large truck pull up outside and stop, its engine idling. Then a there was a knock on the door.

A man wearing a name badge that read HANK smiled at me and held out a clipboard. "Morning, ma'am. If you'll sign right here."

I took the pen and looked down at the page in front of me. "What's this for?"

Hank tapped the page again. "It's an acknowledgment of pickup and delivery."

Two more men bustled past me into the house and into Cannon's bedroom. *What the hell is going on?* They came out carrying the futon.

My stomach churned. Oh fuck, he was really moving out. This was it . . . and it would only be a matter of time before Allie cut me out of her life forever. My heart threatened to stop beating.

My phone rang and I grabbed it from the counter, answering without bothering to check the caller ID.

"Hello?"

"Hey, Paige. It's Cannon."

I'd never been so mortified in my entire life. I wanted to crawl into a hole and die. The need to right this situation before it spiraled even further out of control flared up inside me.

"I am so sorry about last night. I never meant to make you feel awkward." I released a slow, shaky breath, waiting for him to say something.

"So you don't want to fuck me?"

I flinched at his words. Physically, of course I did. But it wasn't worth the emotional turmoil that came with it. Even now, deep in emotional turmoil, my body still reacted to him. But *he* clearly didn't want that. He was repulsed, in fact. God, I was such a fucking idiot.

My voice quivered as I tried to salvage whatever personal pride I could. "I'm so sorry. I never meant to cause any issues. I don't want you to think you have to move out."

"Move out?" His tone was unsure. "Who said anything about moving out?"

"There are men here removing the futon from your bedroom." Crossing the room to the front window, I peeked out. They had a huge white mattress wrapped in plastic and were hauling it from the back of the truck.

"What? Crap, I'm sorry." He sighed. "Let me start over. I got called into the hospital on short notice and forgot to tell you I'm having a bed delivered today. I couldn't sleep on that futon anymore. But they weren't supposed to *take* the damn thing. It's yours."

The men squeezed the mattress through the door and headed for Cannon's room. Suddenly everything made sense. Cannon wasn't mad. He wasn't leaving. In fact, he was making himself more at home.

"Paige? You there?"

"I'm here," I said after a few moments of silence. "Don't worry about the futon. It wouldn't have fit with the bed in there, anyway."

"Are you okay?" he asked. "If you changed your mind about us . . ."

"Did you?" I asked, my heart resuming its gallop for very different reasons than before.

The delivery crew marched past with the bed frame

while I waited for Cannon to answer.

"I've been hard since last night thinking about it. I've wanted you for ten years, Paige."

His admission sent a fresh wave of desire rushing through me. "I didn't change my mind." My voice was uncharacteristically soft.

"I'll be home at seven thirty," he said.

"Dinner?" I asked.

"I take my break at five, and I usually eat then."

"Okay. Seven thirty," I repeated. I'd probably be too nervous to eat anyhow. "I'll see you then."

Once I'd closed the door behind the delivery crew, I wandered back to Cannon's bedroom, feeling almost dazed. The huge king-sized bed took up most of the room, an imposing and ominous sign.

Am I really going to go through with this?

Chapter Ten

Cannon

"Have you decided yet?" Dr. Stinson asked, standing beside me.

I looked down at the options again and frowned. Turkey meat loaf or lasagna. If I was going to rock Paige's world tonight, I wanted to eat light. I didn't want a stomach full of heavy food to impact my performance.

"I might just hit the salad bar," I said, turning to see if the offerings looked wilted.

Dr. Stinson chuckled. "I wasn't asking if you'd decided on dinner. I meant your specialty. You have a clear talent for setting the opposite sex at ease. You'd make a great women's care practitioner."

Grabbing a tray from the stack, I followed him to the salad bar. "I've been thinking more about, uh . . ."

The first thing that jumped into my mind was cardiology. That was what I'd said when Paige had asked. But that was Dr. Stinson's specialty, and I knew if

I said that, he'd start talking my ear off. And I really wanted a break from intense career discussions right now.

"Plastic surgery," I finally blurted.

"Hmm. A tit man, eh?" He chuckled as he heaped his plate with spinach.

I wasn't sure how to take his reaction, but it didn't really matter. It was my decision to make.

Actually, maybe plastic surgery wasn't such a bad idea. With the aging baby-boomer population and Hollywood's obsession with appearance, plastic surgery was a growing field. The money would be damn good. I could build up a nest egg for Mom, then change focus to something like pediatric craniofacial surgery. That would give me a chance to travel abroad—get involved in one of those international charity missions that helped kids born with cleft palates and other facial deformities, providing minor reconstructive surgeries they wouldn't otherwise have access to.

Then again, the prospect of grinding through years of breast augmentations and mommy makeovers sounded like watching paint dry. If it wasn't something I was passionate about, something that interested me, I knew I'd burn out and my work would suffer. And just about any kind of medicine could be put to good use helping the needy. I could pick something else.

When Dr. Stinson cleared his throat, I realized I'd been blocking the tomatoes for almost thirty seconds. Dammit . . . this was exactly my problem. There were too many options, and I had too many factors to consider. I wanted a specialty that wouldn't bore the shit out of me, made enough money to support Mom as well as myself, gave me an excuse to travel, and let me help the needy. Was there a way to have it all? Or would I have to sacrifice some of my priorities?

I piled spring mix onto my plate as my mind wandered to the stack of paperwork I needed to complete before I could leave tonight. I hadn't allowed myself to think about tonight because I couldn't exactly walk around the hospital with a raging hard-on all day. I focused on the work in front of me, never once allowing my mind to wander to the pleasure awaiting me at home. Aside from that one phone call to check on Paige and let her know about the delivery, I'd pushed it all from my mind out of necessity.

But now, with only a couple of hours to go, I was practically itching to get my hands on her. If she'd changed her mind, I might fucking burst. Death by blue balls. If it wasn't already a medical condition, it was about to become one.

• • •

After leaving the hospital, I decided to make a quick stop at the store. Though I wanted to get home as quickly as possible, there were a few necessities I needed. I picked up a box of condoms and a set of sheets for my new bed.

The cashier at Target probably thought I was insane. At the very least, she thought I was getting laid tonight, and she was right. Part of me wanted to really throw her over the edge by adding a can of whipped cream and a package of zip ties to my basket, but I didn't want to give the old lady a heart attack. I was off duty and didn't need another medical emergency on my hands.

It was dark outside by the time I pulled up in front

of Paige's place. A small lamp glowed through the living room window.

I wondered if she'd spent the day as anxious as I'd been. As much as I tried to tell myself it was no big deal, tonight was different from a random hookup. This was Paige, a woman I'd grown up with and secretly lusted after for more than a decade. I hoped that whatever happened wouldn't jeopardize our friendship or her relationship with my sister. But as long as we remembered the "one time only" rule, no one would get hurt, and Allie definitely didn't need to know about this.

Even though I was cursed when it came to sex, and I'd been through hell with countless other women, I wasn't worried about that with Paige. She was mature and responsible, and I believed her when she said there was no way in hell she'd fall in love with me.

Letting myself inside, I found Paige in the dining room. She closed her laptop when she spotted me.

"Hi," she offered, her voice quiet.

I couldn't help but wonder what she was thinking. Was she looking forward to this? Was she just nervous?

Or was she about to call off the whole thing? *Act cool, for fuck's sake . . .*

"Everything okay?" I asked, slipping off my shoes.

Her gaze drifted up and down the front of me, and I realized this was the first time she was seeing me in my scrubs. The soft-washed navy pants were tied low on my waist, and her eyes took their fill.

"Fine," she said, still subdued. She drew her knees up to her chest, looking me over again, but I couldn't read the expression in her eyes.

"I'm going to go take a shower. We'll talk when I get out." And by *talk*, I meant fuck. A man could hope, at least.

After setting my shopping bags down on the counter, I headed for the bathroom. I needed to get the sterile smell of the hospital off my body before I could function.

Standing under the spray of water, I let the steam and heat surround me, working the tension from my muscles. I should have been tired after pulling a ten-hour shift at the hospital, most of it spent on my feet.

Instead, I was keyed up, like a caged animal ready to pounce. I'd wanted Paige for way too long, and the thought of finally having her made me almost dizzy with anticipation. Though, medically speaking, the dizziness could have been from the lack of blood flow to my brain, since it was currently all pumping into my groin, engorging my cock.

After toweling off, I made up the bed with the new sheets. I supposed it could look better with a fluffy comforter and matching pillows and all those things I was terrible at shopping for, but at least it would be comfortable. I wouldn't be crammed onto that narrow futon with my feet hanging off the end any longer. I didn't even want to think about how awful trying to fuck someone for the first time on the damn thing would have been. And not just anyone either, but *Paige*. I wanted to make tonight the best she'd ever had.

Dressed only in a pair of jeans, I left my room to claim her.

Chapter Eleven

Paige

As I sat there listening to the spray of the shower, my jitters multiplied. Cannon was barely ten feet from me, readying himself for our agreed-upon sexual encounter, but now I felt more unsure than ever.

Last night when I'd challenged him—called him out on his cocky opinion that after just one night, women fell hopelessly in love with him—I'd felt sexy, brazen, emboldened by the alcohol, spurred on by the illicit undertones of our late-night conversation. Now, stone-cold sober and with nothing to do all day but think it over, I no longer felt fun and flirty. Every negative possible consequence had replayed through my brain for hours.

Allie would probably never speak to me again if I seduced her brother. Was I really willing to ruin my friendship for a couple of good orgasms? And besides that, Cannon was too young for me. Or rather, I was too old for him. I'd probably disappoint him in the bedroom with a lackluster performance. And what if what he said was true—that he was so amazing in bed, I'd fall in love with him and end up with a broken heart? It was an absurd thought, just his silly superstition at best, but I couldn't get it out of my head.

Unable to sit still any longer, I stood and headed into my bedroom. When I looked into the mirror, I was alarmed to see my cheeks were pink, my neck was splotchy, and my eyes were wild. Shit . . . I was incredibly horny and incredibly scared at the same time, and both emotions were written all over my face.

I blew out a frustrated breath. This wasn't part of the plan.

I tried to give myself a firm pep talk. *I'm a grown woman who can enjoy an evening of primal, sheet-clawing sex like a responsible adult. It's not a big deal.*

Fuck. Who was I kidding? It was a very big deal. I was a nervous wreck, my heart beating a million times a minute. Most of me wanted this, but my reasons were entirely selfish. I'd never been with an amazing lover before. I wanted to see if men like that really existed, wanted to throw caution to the wind for once. But none of that was worth the heartache that would surely follow.

The water shut off, and I heard Cannon moving around. My stomach dropped like a stone. I couldn't do this.

Where was that brave girl who'd propositioned Cannon after learning his dark secret? Gone. Stolen away into the night, along with my courage.

I paced the floor. My home had once been a sacred space, but it now smelled like *him*, bore the distinct markings of *his* presence everywhere I looked. His oversized shoes at the front door. His keys resting in a dish on the counter. A bowl filled with apples on the counter that he took from every morning, sinking his perfectly straight white teeth into the tender flesh with a noise of pleasure.

I knew his habits, knew his scent, but I didn't know what kind of lover he'd be, didn't know the sounds he made when he came. Would he shout with delight, grunt intelligibly, or would he whisper my name as he emptied himself inside? I shivered with curiosity.

I was sick and tired of being the good, mature, responsible adult I knew I was supposed to be. It didn't matter that sleeping with Cannon was wrong—I wanted to sin. Wanted to push myself beyond the safe little bubble I lived inside day in and day out.

Cannon appeared in my doorway, his skin still dewy and flushed from the hot water, his hair damp. His chest was bare and his dark jeans rode enticingly low on his hips. I took a deep breath, preparing to tell him all the reasons why this was a huge mistake.

He stepped up behind me, so close I could smell the citrus-mint bodywash he'd used. Our reflections in the mirror were an experiment in contrasts. He stood a head taller than me, his expression calm and collected. My face was still as red as a tomato, and I looked almost miniature next to him, a feeling I wasn't used to. I wasn't used to any of this; it had been a long time since I'd had a man in my life, let alone in my bedroom.

"Come on." His hand found mine and he laced our fingers together, tugging me away from the mirror and the internal battle I'd waged. "Let's go have a glass of wine."

His voice sent a wave of calm washing over me. I'd been wound tighter than a coil all day, and his suggestion was exactly what I needed. Why was I freaking out? This wasn't life or death. It was two friends hanging out, at least for the moment, and that I could do. *Baby steps, Paige.*

I followed him to the kitchen, where he retrieved a bottle of white wine from the fridge. When he motioned me to the couch, then handed me a glass of wine, I accepted his invitation for both. I felt like a puppet on a string, but going along with his commands actually put me at ease.

I found the conversation flowed easier between us than I would have thought. Travel, business, hobbies, safe topics that still hinted at the things we had in common. Turned out we were both interested in humanitarian work.

I took a deep breath, enjoying both the conversation and the wine. He had grown into a generous and kind man. Maybe it had something to do with being raised by two women. His mom and sister hadn't just fawned all over him—they had built him up, never letting him get complacent, but made sure he knew he was smart and capable, instilling in him a confidence that helped him become the man he was today.

As we sat and talked, sipping our wine, I couldn't help but be reminded of some of the memories we had shared over the years. While Cannon was refilling my wineglass, a smile crossed my lips at a particularly sweet memory . . .

• • •

"Hey! Give me back my backpack, Cannon!" Placing one hand on my slim hip, I'd held the other out toward him, trying to muster as much authority as I could.

I was twelve and had recently started my first period. My pink Hello Kitty backpack held my stash of pads in a secret compartment inside. The last thing I wanted was Allie's little brother finding them. *Gross!* I'd be mortified.

"My mom said I'm the man of the house. It's my 'sponsibility to carry all the bags, open all the doors, and treat women with respect." He straightened his posture, hoisting my backpack higher onto his slight shoulder.

Ugh. Cannon could be a real pain in the behind sometimes. We were waiting outside the school for my mom to pick us up, and he was loaded down with not only his Captain America backpack, but Allie's bag and lunchbox too. He looked like a pack mule.

"Give it here." I motioned again. "I can carry my own bag." My grandma said I didn't need a man to do anything for me, and besides, Cannon wasn't even a man yet. He was only eight years old.

His gaze flashed over to Allie, and she nodded once.

"Fine," he said, handing my bag over with reluctance. "Here you go."

Relieved, I clutched the bag to my chest, a little surprised that I wasn't actually mad at Cannon. As far as boys went, he wasn't all that bad . . .

• • •

"You doing better?" Cannon asked, his gaze moving over me.

I bit my lip and nodded. "I guess it was obvious I was freaking out before, huh?"

"We don't have to do this."

"What?" I murmured.

"Any of this. We can go back to pretending this chemistry buzzing between us doesn't exist. I won't pressure you."

His words should have calmed me, but instead they irritated, grating against my skin. I didn't *want* to pretend anymore. I was sick of being a coward and calling it caution, prudence, restraint. That was the old Paige. Afraid to try anything new, living inside a bubble. On the slippery side of thirty and still single—with a stray dog instead of the stereotypical cat, but still, just as sheltered and pathetic. The new Paige was adventuresome and daring. At least, she wanted to be.

"No." I shook my head. "This was my idea. You're not pressuring me." I leaned forward and set my wineglass on the table in front of us. "I'm just not sure how to . . . start."

"That's my job, princess."

Princess? I didn't hate that nickname as much as I probably should have. I hadn't been anyone's princess in a long time. *Or ever*, as the little voice inside my head reminded me. Cannon had called me that growing up, but it was meant in fun, to tease and taunt. This new, adult version of the boy I remembered was filled with surprises.

His eyes were dark and filled with unspoken passion. And his full, perfect mouth was tilted in a slight smile. He was so ridiculously sexy that my stomach tied into knots whenever I just looked at him.

I was still nervous. But come on . . . this was *Cannon*. I'd known him for more than twenty years. He wasn't going to hurt me, or disappear in the morning and never call again. We'd share this house for the next couple of months, probably make pancakes on Saturday mornings and laugh about the time we got it on. We'd get the attraction out of our systems and move on. It was merely scratching an itch.

He placed his wineglass next to mine, then leaned closer, tracing his fingertips lightly over my jaw before drawing my face toward his.

This was it.

He was going to kiss me.

It was time to show him that I was more than capable of a one-night stand without falling in love— either that or scurry back to my room, alone and afraid. Those were my two choices. Unless the fire alarm decided to sound in the next four seconds, his full lips were going to be on mine.

Making the split-second decision to put my money where my mouth was, I leaned in.

Cannon smiled against my lips, in no rush to claim his prize. Maybe because he knew it was already his. Maybe because, unlike most men, he understood the virtues of slowing down. We both wanted this, but delaying gratification would make it that much better when we did finally get there.

Slowly, his lips moved against mine, parting so our tongues could tentatively touch. It was electric.

Deepening the kiss, his mouth fused over mine, taking all I had to give. His hand cradled my jaw, his tongue tasted of wine, and I realized I'd never been kissed like this. So possessively. So completely. I was hardly inexperienced . . . but whatever I'd been doing before, I couldn't call it real kissing anymore. With careful licks against my tongue, Cannon taught me how to kiss all over again.

Holy shit! I'm making out with Cannon Roth. This should have felt strange and utterly foreign. My brain should have been screaming *Abort! Abort!* Instead, it was the most natural thing in the world. Our tongues moved together as though they'd spent years training for this exact moment. Lust mixed with pleasure rolled through my veins.

Pulling back a few inches, he smirked at me again. "You still with me?"

Eagerly, I nodded, drugged with my desire for him. If he could make me feel this out of control from one kiss, I was almost scared to find out what the rest of the night had in store.

He placed my hand against the bulge in his pants. It

was hot and hard, and made my insides clench. "Do you feel that, Paige?"

I swallowed a groan. He felt so warm and solid beneath my palm. "Y-yes."

"Do you want me inside you?" he murmured, trailing kisses up my neck while I continued rubbing his erection through his jeans.

"God, yes."

His warm, silky chuckle vibrated against my skin. "Good, because I've wanted to fuck you since I was sixteen years old. But tonight's not about me. I'm going to make sure this is good for you. Do you want that?"

"Yes. Of course."

"Then you need to trust me."

For a second, I wondered if I could do that. Totally give over control? I was an independent woman, and what if he was into some kinky stuff? I pushed the thoughts away. I would suspend judgment . . . for now.

"I do trust you."

"Good girl." His lips met mine once again, kissing me until my body pulsed in a lustful frenzy. After a few moments, he broke away. Reluctantly, I pulled my hand away from his cock and opened my eyes.

"Are you absolutely sure you want to do this? If my track record is any indication, this won't end well."

To my wine-buzzed, lust-clouded brain, his warning to stay away was about as effective as one of those "enter only if you're eighteen" notices on a porn site.

"I want this. I want you." I looked right into his emerald-colored eyes as I spoke, hoping he could feel the sheer desire in my voice.

"Then let's take this to the bedroom."

Rising from the couch, I followed him down the hall. "Is that why you got the bed?"

"Yes. That, and I didn't exactly fit on the futon."

My heart pounded as we entered his bedroom. He'd made up the massive king-sized bed with new sheets, and his masculine scent hung in the air all around us.

"Turn around," he murmured.

I faced the full-length mirror that was mounted on the wall as Cannon stood behind me. The room was cast in shadows, but there was enough light to watch his large hands move up my sides, over my hips, my waist, all the way up until he lifted my hair from my shoulder, then placed a tender kiss at the base of my neck. Little chill bumps erupted, dancing down my spine.

Transfixed, I watched his hands move from my neck to my shoulders, down to cup my achy breasts.

My breathing went shallow as his fingertips traced my nipples.

"You have beautiful breasts, Paige."

His thumbs grazed the firm peaks of my nipples, and I sucked in a breath.

"You like your nipples stimulated?"

I arched my back in reply, leaning my head against his chest, pushing my breasts forward into his hands.

"Good to know, princess." He kissed the side of my neck. "I'd love to fuck these pretty tits sometime."

He pulled my shirt off over my head and let it drop to the floor. My chest heaved as he unfastened my bra and dropped it next to my shirt. In the mirror, a topless me stood against the backdrop of Cannon's broad, muscled body. His fingers, strong and certain, traced up my rib cage as I watched.

If I'd thought it felt good before, his large, warm palms against the naked flesh of my breasts was almost too much. My breath shuddered, and sparks zinged straight from my nipples to between my legs. But Cannon didn't torture me for long. His eyes were dark and hooded as his hands moved lower, sliding inside the front of my pants, into my underwear.

I gasped at the very welcome invasion. His fingers made contact with my slick flesh, and I bit back a moan.

"No," he said. "Don't hold back. Let me hear you."

He stroked me again, making feather-soft circles against my clit, and I whimpered in pleasure, both relieved that the wait was over and impatient for more.

"That's right," he said, encouraging me. "You like watching me touch you, princess?"

I did, but I couldn't string together the words to tell him, couldn't form a coherent thought right now if my life depended on it. His skilled hands knew all the spots, and just the right pressure and speed to deliver maximum pleasure.

Leaning back into his solid form, I succumbed and let the pleasure wash over me, pushing my hips forward to grant him even greater access. He rewarded me by sliding one thick finger inside me. Another needy cry escaped me. I wasn't the type to climax quickly—the few lovers I'd been with in the past had had to work at it—but somehow, after just a few short minutes, Cannon had me poised right on the edge. That dangerous place where I'd splinter into a million fragments and burst apart.

Surrounded by his warm muscle and rich, masculine scent, I lost all sense of modesty, moaning out loud as he slid his finger in and out, watching him watch me. It was incredibly erotic.

"You're beautiful. It's a privilege to touch you."

I could have melted at his darkly seductive tone. It was clear he meant it; his breathing was ragged and his erection pressed as hard as steel into my lower back.

With one hand between my legs, he caressed my breasts with the other. His mouth burned against my neck. "Are you going to come for me, gorgeous girl?" he whispered against my skin.

I shuddered in his arms, coming apart at the seams as my release tore through me. White light burst beyond my vision, blood thundering in my ears as my body clenched almost violently around his fingers. Blinded by pleasure, nothing else existed for me but his soft touches, gentle kisses, and dirty whispers.

Coming down from my high, I sagged against him, grateful when his strong arms wrapped around me.

Cannon spun me around to face him and lifted me up, holding me tightly against his chest while he walked us toward the bed, where he stripped me of my pants and underwear.

"I've got you," he said, placing me in the center of the pillow-top mattress.

Boneless and relaxed, I smiled at him shyly, watching as he pushed his pants and boxers down, freeing that thick, gorgeous cock I'd dreamed about since the night I'd run into him naked in the hallway. I almost groaned at the beautiful sight. He was exquisite. I wanted to touch him, to taste him, to hear him moan with pleasure.

His hand found his cock and he stroked slowly once, twice, my core tightening all over again as I watched him. "You ready for more?"

I nodded. "Come here."

He grabbed a condom from the top of the desk and rolled it on with practiced ease. Joining me on the bed, Cannon positioned himself between my parted thighs. But rather than drive into me with a powerful thrust like I expected, he drew out the moment, kissing me deeply and rubbing his length over my slick center, taking his time, letting the desire build even hotter, higher.

It was the sweetest form of torture I'd ever experienced. My body was still reeling from my first release, my core simultaneously hypersensitive and pulsing with renewed need. His thick cock ground against my wet, ready center.

He was taking his time. I wasn't sure why that surprised me. When we agreed to a one-night stand, I'd imagined us climbing between the sheets and getting down to business. I'd thought it would be little more than a meaningless fuck, but boy was I wrong. Delightfully wrong. I hadn't counted on the kissing and the foreplay and the dirty whispers breathed against my naked skin.

I gripped his hips, flashing him a playful smile. "Fuck me, big boy."

"With pleasure, beautiful." He drew back, finding the right angle, then pressed forward slowly so that the broad tip of him entered me.

I winced at the intrusion and Cannon paused, allowing me to adjust. Apparently it had been longer than I thought, and my body was all W-T-F.

Concern knitted his brow as he looked down at me. "You're pretty tight," he said softly.

"Sorry," I gritted out.

"Don't be. You're perfect the way you are."

I swallowed the lump in my throat. I couldn't remember the last time someone had told me that. I sure as hell didn't feel perfect. I felt confused and so full—of emotion, of him—that I might fall apart so completely I'd never be put back together the same way ever again.

"You need a minute?" he whispered.

Burying my face in the warm crook of his neck, I nodded. *How embarrassing!*

I took a deep breath and tried to relax. I knew Cannon was primed and ready for this, knew I needed to relax and let him in. This was my idea, after all. Another deep inhale, and I parted my knees further.

Just then, a series of loud knocks rang out against my front door.

What the hell? No one ever came over unannounced. A wave of frustration seized me. *Really, universe? Right goddamn now?*

Cannon looked just as startled as I felt. "Are you

expecting someone?"

I met his eyes and shook my head. "Of course not."

Everything was quiet for a second, and I figured whoever it was had the wrong house and they'd moved on.

"Need to fuck you." Cannon groaned, gripping my ass roughly in one palm. I knew his restraint was hanging by a thread, and that sent my heart racing.

"Yes," I moaned.

He pushed in one inch more and we both held our breath, waiting for me to adjust. The pain soon ebbed, giving way to a sweet, satisfying stretch, and I parted my thighs to signal him deeper . . .

The silence evaporated as the knocking started again, louder this time. And it didn't let up. Someone was pounding at my door like a lunatic.

My eyes widened and found Cannon's. What a fucking awkward situation. With just the wide flared head of his cock inside me, there we lay, our limbs intertwined, our hearts pounding, like a porno left on pause.

Of all the absurd situations to find myself in—being interrupted by pounding at the door, when all I wanted was him pounding into me.

He groaned in frustration, placing his lips against my throat. "Don't even fucking think about it."

"I have to. Just let me see who it is, and I'll send them away. I promise. I just don't want my neighbors to call the police."

He pulled out of me, achingly slowly, letting out a hiss. "Fuck."

I patted his chest and smiled at him.

Gripping my wrist, he held me firm and met my eyes. "Hurry."

His cock stood tall, proud, and tempting against his stomach, and I gave it one last look of longing as I threw my shirt on over my head and shimmied into my discarded jeans.

Fuck! Leaving my damp panties on the floor, I

rushed from the bedroom toward the front door. The motherfucking zombie apocalypse better be here for all the racket going on at my doorstep.

Glancing through the peephole, I saw that it was Allie.

Chapter Twelve

Paige

"You better be dead or dying." I pulled open the door with a huff.

Allie was standing at my front door, her fist still poised for pounding. If she only knew what she'd interrupted, what was going on inside the bedroom a mere twenty feet away . . .

What the hell? Hot shame burned through me at the sight of Allie's bright red face, streaked with tears and the remnants of her mascara.

"Oh God, Al. What's going on?" I pulled her inside, and she practically launched herself into my arms with a broken sob.

It took several minutes of coaxing the words out of her, waiting patiently as she gulped and hiccupped, to understand that she'd had a fight with James.

I led her to the couch and told her to sit while I grabbed a box of tissues. It wasn't a lie, but it wasn't the whole truth either. I sped toward Cannon's room to tell him to get his ass dressed and presentable ASAP.

"Cannon!" I whispered, peeking in through the open door. He was still lying in the center of the bed, naked, with his hard cock jutting up on his belly. "Allie's here," I whisper-yelled.

"Fuck!" He jumped up from the bed, grabbing his pants from the floor and yanking them on at lightning speed.

I winced at the idea of how it must feel to stuff that huge erection back inside its tight denim prison. *Eeee.* Not good, I imagined.

But I had no time to linger. I rushed off to grab the tissues and met Allie back in the living room. Thankfully, she gave no indication of suspecting that her brother was just inside me not thirty seconds ago. *Fucking hell!* I was a terrible friend.

Handing her a wad of tissues, I sat down beside her to wait as she blew her nose and got herself under control. It took several minutes of deep breathing.

I took her hand. "What in the world happened?"

Even if I wasn't a fan, Allie loved James. Whatever it was would surely blow over in a day or two, once they both had a chance to cool down.

"He's been cheating on me for months."

Or maybe not. "What are you talking about?" I asked.

Cannon strolled out of the bedroom looking collected and put together. Thank God. He met my eyes quickly as he gave Allie a hug. "You okay, sis?"

She sucked in a breath and nodded once. "I will be once I get that lying, cheating sack of shit out of my life."

"What happened?" I asked, trying to ignore my body's response to Cannon's proximity. *Pesky pheromones.* It had been *way* too long since I'd had any attention from the opposite sex. I would have to rectify that; otherwise I'd be jumping Cannon's bones every chance I got. I made a mental note to sign up for that stupid dating app Allie had been hounding me about the first chance I got.

Allie took a deep breath. "James has been having

an affair." She spoke calmly, but her expression was pained and her hands were fisted in her lap. "It was all a lie—all the times he said he had to work late, or go into the office on a Sunday. He's been carrying on with another woman for months now. A divorcée with two kids . . . not that it fucking matters."

All the breath whooshed from my lungs. That was the last thing I'd expected to hear.

"I saw some text messages on his phone. I wasn't snooping; it was sitting right there on the counter. And when I confronted him, he admitted everything."

"Fuck that." Cannon rose to his feet, heading toward the door.

"Where are you going?" Allie whined.

He pulled his shoes on and grabbed his car keys from the counter. "I'm going over there to beat his ass."

Allie jumped up and grabbed her brother's arm. "Stop and think for two seconds. As much as I'd love for you to deliver that beat-down, it's not worth you getting in trouble or messing up your hands. You're going to be a world-renowned surgeon one day. And that makes me much happier than you kicking his ass ever would."

Cannon's eyes narrowed on hers and he released a deep breath, his nostrils flaring.

I'd never seen him so angry. Sure, I'd seen his protective side a million times growing up, but not with this much ferocity. It was kind of fucking hot.

After a few tense moments, Allie succeeded in talking him out of his plan, and Cannon sat down beside me once again. The fun, flirty mood we'd shared earlier was gone, driven out by the angry tension that filled the room.

Over the next hour, Cannon and I took turns building Allie up, telling her she was better off without James, and bolstering her self-confidence. I wasn't certain it was working, but at least Allie was no longer crying, and she was nodding along with what we were saying.

I was careful not to admit that I'd never liked James. Part of me knew—with utmost disgust, but still—that it was possible he'd come crawling back, say all the right things, and they'd patch things up. If that happened, revealing my dislike for him would forever drive a wedge between Allie and me.

Cannon had no such qualms, repeatedly telling Allie that she could do better and that James was nothing more than a piece of trash. I silently cheered him on.

Soon we were drinking wine, munching on popcorn, and watching the latest horror movie that we'd rented. While Allie was still emotionally devastated, she had recovered enough to put on a brave face. She'd already texted James and told him to make sure that he and his things were gone by morning. I was immensely proud of her.

"Love you, Al," I said, giving her hand a squeeze.

Sometime later, I woke to a large hand nudging my shoulder. My eyes fluttered open, and I found Cannon standing over me. Through my sleepy haze, I noticed the TV was off, all the snacks and drinks had been cleaned up, and Allie lay asleep on the couch with a blanket tucked around her.

"Come on," he whispered, offering me his hand.

I accepted, letting him pull me to my feet. "I think I nodded off during that last movie."

"You and Allie both." Placing one arm around my waist, he smiled. "I've got you."

He helped me to my bedroom but stopped at the threshold, as though he didn't want to invade my space. A knot of worry formed inside me. Earlier he'd been so eager—we both had. But now things felt murky.

"So, what happens next?" I asked.

"Allie's tough. I'm sure she'll be fine."

"I wasn't talking about Allie and James. I meant us."

"Oh, right. You mean . . ." His eyebrows jumped up flirtatiously.

"Yes."

"That was probably the worst case of blue balls I've ever had, but I get it. My sister needed you. You're a good friend."

Oh yeah, some great friend. I was practically riding her little brother a few hours ago.

I nodded, though, and released a heavy sigh. "Maybe a rain check?"

"If that's what you want," he murmured, leaning down to press a soft kiss against my cheek. "But I'm working nights the next few days. You may not see much of me."

"Okay. Good night," I whispered, heading into my bedroom.

I had no idea how our half-finished encounter would change the atmosphere around the house, or when this rain check might be cashed in. But what happened next was totally unexpected.

Chapter Thirteen

Paige

Cannon hadn't been lying when he'd said I wouldn't see much of him this week. It was Thursday and our paths had crossed only twice while he was coming and going. He worked all night at the hospital, then slept all day. We occasionally left each other Post-it notes around the house, silly little things like the strict orders I gave him to stay away from my Chinese leftovers, or the note he'd left letting me know we were out of almond milk but he'd pick up more.

While I was busy not seeing Cannon, it gave me time to stew over my decision to sleep with him. My stomach had been tied in knots all week over what to do. Clearly, our failed attempt at sex was a sign from the universe. Sleeping with Allie's little brother had been a terrible idea, after all. Horniness had clouded my judgment. I just needed to get laid, and I had a plan for how to take care of that. One that wouldn't ruin my longest-standing friendship, or turn things weird with my new and decidedly male roommate.

It was dark outside, and Cannon was gone for the evening. As I sat with a glass of wine in one hand and my phone in the other, I scrolled through photos of guys the dating app had matched me with.

Allie had worn me down; I'd finally signed up. She'd been true to her word and had thrown James and all his shit out of her apartment, so I felt like letting her have this small victory was the right thing to do. Spending so much of this week alone, feeling lonely and sorry for myself, had only pushed me harder in that direction.

Taking another sip of chardonnay, I clicked on the envelope icon in the upper right corner of the screen. I had two unread messages—the first was an automated message welcoming me to the site, but the other was from someone named Daniel. His message was brief and playful.

DANIEL: *You look like trouble. ;)*

I smiled and clicked on his photo to enlarge it. The

brown-haired, brown-eyed man in the photo was decent-looking, I supposed. Cannon was much hotter with his messy sandy hair and huge biceps and magnetic smile. But Cannon wasn't here right now, and he was off-limits anyway. I clicked REPLY and typed a return message.

After another glass of wine and several messages back and forth, I was actually having a good time talking to Daniel. He lived one town over and worked as a financial analyst. He was thirty-two and had never been married, and his messages made me laugh. But then Daniel asked me out to dinner tomorrow night, and even though I was free, I hesitated. Part of me felt strange going out with someone else when Cannon's cock had been *this* close to penetrating me only a handful of days ago. I told Daniel I would think about it and let him know tomorrow, and then went to plug my phone in to charge in the kitchen.

I hadn't expected to be asked out on a date so quickly. Allie was right about one thing, that dating site certainly worked fast. But seriously, what was I supposed to do when a decent-looking man who seemed nice and normal suggested dinner? Say no thanks, I have a rain check to sleep with my new roommate? That would be crazy. I doubted Cannon would have turned down female attention simply because we might, or might not, be rescheduling our failed fuck session.

After filling a glass with tap water, I stood at the sink, taking small sips. It wasn't like Cannon would even know about the date. He was working nights, and I'd probably be gone and back before he knew anything. Not that I needed to hide Daniel from him—I was perfectly in my rights to date. Wasn't I?

I dumped the rest of the glass into the sink, then grabbed my phone and replied to Daniel, letting him know we were on for tomorrow night. Having that settled should have felt good, but instead it only left me feeling more confused.

As I went to get ready for bed, I hoped this weekend would bring me some clarity on what to do about Cannon. I had an unhealthy fascination with him, and didn't see that ending anytime soon with us living under the same roof.

• • •

Daniel was a dud.

Okay, that wasn't totally fair. Dinner was good and the conversation was fine, but Daniel and I simply didn't have any chemistry. It was like talking to my cousin or a coworker. There was no spark, no electricity buzzing between us—not like my conversations with Cannon.

I removed my napkin from my lap, wiped my mouth one last time, and set it on the table beside me.

"Are you finished?" Daniel asked.

I nodded and signaled the server to bring our check. I'd been discreetly checking my phone under the table. The more wine I drank at dinner, the better idea it seemed to try to get home in time to see Cannon. And if we left now, I had twenty-three minutes before he left for his night shift at the hospital.

Daniel nabbed the check as soon as the server dropped it off. "I've got this. Thank you for joining me for dinner."

"Are you sure? I don't mind splitting it," I offered.

He nodded. "It's my pleasure."

I smiled at him. He really was a nice guy.

While he settled the bill, I used the restroom, checking my appearance in the mirror. Satisfied that my hair and makeup were still in place and I didn't have any food stuck in my teeth, I met Daniel at the front of the restaurant.

He drove me home, talking to me yet again about his work as a financial analyst.

I held back a yawn. Surely two people could find more to talk about than spreadsheets and investments. But I didn't care enough to try, so I nodded along.

"Thank you for tonight," I said when he stopped at the curb in front of my house.

He put his car into park and hopped out, coming around to open my door. He was a little old-fashioned, insisting on picking me up, paying for dinner, and opening doors. But I kind of liked that in a man.

"I'll walk you up to your door," he suggested.

I nodded, following him up the stairs to my small

porch, and plastered a polite smile onto my lips while he finished his story about last quarter's earnings statements.

Come on! Cannon's car was still parked out front, which meant he was still inside.

But then Daniel leaned in, his garlic breath fanning over my cheek, and I did the only thing I could think of. I brought my knee up swiftly, connecting with the spot between Daniel's legs.

"*Oompf!*" He doubled over, his forehead crashing into my nose.

"Ow." My nose stung where I'd been struck.

"Why the hell did you do that?" Daniel barked.

I had no answer. Panicked, I guessed. When I pinched the bridge of my nose, my hand came away red. *Shit.* My nose was bleeding and Daniel was still bent in half, clutching his crotch.

"I . . . I'm so sorry," I stammered.

The door flew open and Cannon's gaze raked over me, then Daniel, and back to me. Specifically, the blood running from my nose. His eyes turned murderous as he set his sights back on Daniel.

"What the fuck did you do to her?" he growled, stalking closer.

Grabbing Cannon's firm bicep, I stepped between them. "It was just a misunderstanding. He didn't hit me. We bumped heads."

Cannon didn't stop glaring daggers at Daniel.

I found it hard to blame Cannon for disbelieving an unbelievable situation. Who the hell fails so hard at kissing they come away with a bloody nose? God, I was a hot mess.

"Come on, Paige. Let's go inside." Cannon offered me his hand and I took it, letting him draw me away from the man on my porch.

"You can have her, buddy. Good fucking luck!" Daniel called, already stomping down the steps and back toward his car.

Once inside, Cannon turned on the light in the foyer, tilting my chin and inspecting me carefully.

"Christ," he swore under his breath. I could see the tick in his jaw as he bit down, his gaze still tracing my form. "Does this hurt?" He pressed a spot on my forehead.

I shook my head, dislodging his hand. "No, really, I'm fine. It's just a little bloody nose."

"Come sit down." Taking my hand, he led me into the living room and stood over me while I lowered myself onto the couch.

"Don't you have to get to work?" I asked.

He was dressed in his scrubs, baby blue this time, and *damn*, the man even made drawstring pants look sexy. The cotton shirt had the slightest V-neck—just a notch, really—but the smooth, tanned skin and hollow of his throat visible in that notch was everything. That tiny peek, that tease of bare skin, was a million times sexier than all of Daniel's bland flirting combined. I wanted to lick it, suck on it, sniff it . . .

Holy shit, Paige, calm down. I hadn't felt so out of control since I was a teenager. I seriously needed to get a grip—and no, not on Cannon's dick. But my hormones held me hostage. I couldn't help but watch his butt flex as he retreated to the bathroom.

Seconds later, he returned with a box of tissues, withdrew several, and handed them to me. "Yes, but first I need to be sure you're okay. I'm not leaving for the night when you could have a concussion."

I snorted, holding a wad of tissue against my nose. "I don't have a concussion. It was nothing. Clumsiness combined with wine and a dash of self-preservation."

He sat down beside me, stroking my cheek softly. "Are you telling me the truth? You just bumped heads? He didn't . . . ?"

I tried to nod and shake my head at the same time. "He tried to kiss me and I panicked."

"Why did you panic?" Cannon's gaze was hard and locked on mine.

His attention felt amazing, the rough pads of his fingertips, the worry in his eyes. I wanted to stay in this moment forever. My heart thumped steadily under his concerned gaze. If this was what it was like to be a patient of Dr. Cannon Roth, sign me the fuck up.

I swallowed. "I didn't want to kiss him. I only went out on that stupid date because . . ."

"Because why?" His posture was tense, but his words were soft.

Because he wasn't you. Because I'm more hung up on you than I have any right to be.

I swallowed. "Because we never got to finish what we started."

"We didn't get to fuck, so you moved on and now you're dating."

His direct eye contact was too much, and I found my gaze drifting to the floor between my feet. God, when he said it like that, I sounded like an asshole.

"We dodged a bullet, right?" I meant it to sound calm and certain, but my voice came out shakier than I intended. Clearing my throat, I started again. "We got interrupted. We never even officially had sex, and now we can both move on. It would have been a huge mistake, and besides, according to you, I would have fallen hopelessly in love with you and it would have ended terribly."

"If you're too much of a pussy to finish what we started, fine by me, but don't equate us getting interrupted to dodging a bullet. It would have been fun, and you know it."

My cheeks heated. Oh, did I ever. I hadn't been able to stop thinking about him once. The way he'd felt with his muscular frame atop mine, the restrained power in his hips when he pressed forward the slightest bit, the way he hissed when he felt how tight I was . . . I shivered just thinking of it.

"Is this what you really want? To date some schmuck you met online?" Cannon asked.

"Yes. It's what I really want." It was a lie. A total fucking lie that felt bitter on my tongue.

As much as I craved the perks that came with a relationship—affection, intimacy, support, sex—I was even more terrified about giving my heart to anyone. What if they turned out to be like James, and I ended up destroyed in the end?

But I wouldn't say that to Cannon. He had been a fun fling, a distraction, but he couldn't be anything more. He had grand plans he needed to focus on, and Allie would never stand for it. Besides, I was about ninety-nine percent sure that Cannon was not at all interested in a steady girlfriend.

His hand fell away from my cheek, and his full lips parted as he appraised me. "I can't have you going out with a man who doesn't know how to properly kiss a woman without it ending in a bloody nose."

I should have said something snappy like, *You don't get to decide who I date.* But what came out was, "That's true."

The blush on my cheeks spread. Not only did I feel like an idiot, but now Cannon knew just how much I was lusting after him—if he hadn't known already. For a grown damned woman, I felt totally childish and immature.

"I'm going to be late to work. We'll figure this out tomorrow."

I nodded and watched him rise to his feet, my heart still galloping. Figure this out? Like his massive dick and my overly tight you-know-what coming together was some math equation.

He bent down and brushed one hand along my cheek. "You sure you're okay?"

"I'll be fine." *As soon as this shame and self-pity wears off.*

With one last worried glance cast in my direction, Cannon nodded and headed for the door. "Call me if you need anything, and don't forget to lock up."

Placing my head in my hands, I let out a long sigh. I'd ruined the only date I'd had in over a year and rushed home for nothing. I still didn't know where I stood with Cannon, and now I wasn't going to find out.

Adulthood was just as shitty as everyone said. Except not if you were Cannon Roth. He still had that bright and shiny hope radiating from his emerald eyes. Belief that something great was out there on the horizon waiting for him—and maybe it was.

I wanted to bask in that feeling, to linger in his presence in the hope that some of his optimism and passion wore off on me. Because right now? My life was a total shit show.

Chapter Fourteen

Cannon

It shouldn't have, but Paige going out on that date really pissed me off. I knew I had little right to be angry; she didn't owe me anything, and I'd barely even seen her in the week since our near miss.

But I couldn't help the jealous rage that boiled through my veins when I found her on the porch with that guy. And when I thought he'd hurt her? I wanted to pummel his face in. I still didn't know if it was like she'd claimed, that they'd just bumped heads when he tried to kiss her, but Paige had never lied to me, as far as I knew.

On my drive to the hospital, I called to check on Allie, pleased that she'd kicked that scumbag James to the curb. My life these days consisted of obligations. I worked, slept, hit the gym, studied, checked in on my mom and sister, worked some more. Lather. Rinse. Repeat. I knew there was a purpose, knew there was a reason I was doing this, but fuck, some days it was hard to remember what that reason was.

Tonight the urge to stay home and make sure Paige was okay was stronger than ever. Just say *fuck it* to my never-ending responsibilities and hang out with someone who made me feel comfortable, at ease, and a whole lot turned on.

I wouldn't push Paige for more, wouldn't push her on the sex we were supposed to have. Did I want to finish what we started? Of course I did. Getting interrupted that night had almost killed me. Paige had been so hot, so tight, so responsive.

I wanted her. *Badly*. It didn't help that I'd fantasized about having her for the last decade. Pulling out before I was even really inside her had been the worst form of torture imaginable. Everything inside me was screaming *no* from the second I'd heard that pounding at the door. Then less than a week after I'd had her in my bed, wet and eager, she was out on a date with some other guy.

But I had to suck it up and go to work. Even though I knew tonight's shift would crawl by, since I'd be counting the hours until I could see her this weekend.

Chapter Fifteen

Paige

A whispered voice at the edge of my bed woke me. "Paige?"

"Yeah?" I slurred, blinking in the darkness. The only light came from the hallway, casting the room in shadows.

Cannon's shadowy form stood a few feet from where I slept. He said nothing, just crossed the room and sat beside me on the bed.

Groggy and confused, I lifted my head. "What time is it?"

"About one in the morning. We were overstaffed and slow, so they sent me home early."

That didn't explain what he was doing in my bedroom. I blinked at him slowly.

"I just wanted to make sure you were okay," he continued.

It took me a second to remember what had happened earlier. I'd gone on a date with Daniel the Douche and ended up with a bloody nose. It hadn't hurt much, so the blood had surprised me.

"I'm fine," I said.

Cannon's warm palm found my cheek, and he brushed the hair back from my face. "Couldn't sleep till I made sure you were all right."

I swallowed, leaning into his touch, enjoying the way his strong fingers felt moving through my hair, stroking my scalp. Letting my eyes slip closed, I murmured something unintelligible, and Cannon chuckled.

"Just rest, princess. Sorry I woke you."

I felt his lips on my forehead, and then the mattress shifted as he rose from the bed. Missing his warm, masculine touch almost immediately, I reached out toward him.

"Don't go. Not yet," I whispered.

Normally, I would have been too ashamed to say

that. I would have forced myself to be an adult and let him leave. But deep in the night, in the pitch-black darkness, I could ask for what I wanted. I didn't have to look at his face or worry about what he saw on mine. Nothing that happened between midnight and sunrise counted; I could hide behind the strange darkness that blanketed the world when everyone we knew was asleep. And in the daylight, I could write off this slipup as a dream.

He hesitated for the briefest of moments, and I moved over, making room in the bed.

Then he climbed in beside me, lying down on top of the covers, and in his calming presence, I fell back to sleep almost instantly.

Chapter Sixteen

Cannon

I woke up with a face full of hair and a massive erection. *The hell?*

Combing back the honey-colored tresses with my fingers, I blinked open one eye and saw that I was still in bed with Paige. I'd fallen asleep listening to her deep, steady breaths, enjoying the closeness long after I should have moved to my own room. It usually took me forever to unwind enough to fall asleep after a shift, but lying there in the darkness and listening to her breathe, I was able to break through the day's tension and just relax.

But what had started innocently, with me on top of the blankets, somehow had ended with me stripped down to my boxer briefs and under the covers with Paige. I had no idea what time it was, only that it was barely daylight. The T-shirt she'd slept in had ridden up to expose her pink cotton panties printed all over with little donuts, complete with colorful sprinkles.

A wry smile tugged at my mouth. She was sexy without even trying. Most women weren't sexy first thing in the morning, but there was no black makeup smeared under her eyes, no death-breath emanating from her in an unpleasant wave. There was nothing but soft, sweet female to worship and indulge in.

She stretched her long, toned legs under the blankets, letting out a squeak, then opened her eyes. "Morning, Cannon."

"Hi, princess."

"You stayed." She smiled shyly.

I hadn't meant to, honestly, but no way was I telling her that. I couldn't stand to see that smile chased away just yet.

"Yeah, I fell asleep. Is that okay?" I rubbed one hand over my hair and smiled back at her.

"I didn't take you for the cuddling type."

"I can be." I'd never been the type to sleep over or cuddle before in my life. But I didn't want to think about that right now. "Come here." I opened my arms, urging her closer, and Paige lifted the corner of the sheet to slide over.

Then she jerked back. "Shit."

"What is it?" I followed her gaze down to my crotch. *Christ!* My cock was so hard and eager, standing so tall, that he was peeking at her from the top of my briefs.

Her shy smile fell away, and she bit her lip.

"Ignore it. Come here," I said again, encouraging her.

She obeyed, cautiously scooting closer until her body was against mine.

"Is that just a normal biological thing, or are you turned on right now?" she asked, her voice hesitant.

"A little of both?"

I was turned on *as fuck*, but I didn't want to scare her away or have her thinking I was going to stuff her full of all eight inches . . . unless she was damn sure that was what she wanted. And after last night, I had no idea if it was.

Uneasy laughter was followed by a pat to my chest. "Okay, Cannon."

She snuggled closer, placing her head next to mine on the pillow, her body touching mine from shoulder to hip. I held her there, enjoying the feel of her warm softness. *Perfection.*

I wondered if she was thinking the same thing I was. This was the first time we'd been together since our failed attempt at sex.

"I'm actually a little hungry," I admitted, gripping her hip and tugging her ass back until my dick was nestled right between those soft, plump cheeks.

She let out a strangled noise.

"For donuts," I continued, enjoying this way too much.

"D-donuts?" she stuttered. I didn't know if she was thinking about the fact that I usually ate healthy, or was remembering the panties she wore.

The hand I'd rested on her hip drifted lower, and I rubbed my thumb over the fabric of her panties. She looked down and awareness blossomed in her.

"Can I have a taste, princess?"

I wouldn't do a damn thing without her consent. If she wanted this as badly as I did, she was going to have to tell me. I needed her words. Needed to know she was dying for this like I was. Only then would I cross the line we could never uncross.

"I . . . I haven't showered."

The meaning behind her words hit me like a punch to the gut, and for the briefest of moments, I got angry. I wasn't sure what kind of men she'd been with before, or if they'd made her feel self-conscious about her scent or taste. But her sentiment was foreign to me. No man would ever stop his girl from blowing him because he thought his cock wasn't worthy of her mouth. No, he'd shove it down her eager throat, taking pleasure in the way his musk marked her. If she wanted him dirty, then by God, she would have him.

Did Paige really have such deep hang-ups about her body . . . or was it because she was afraid of displeasing *me* specifically?

I took a deep breath through my nostrils, forcing myself to calm down. It didn't really matter why she'd shied away. It was my duty to reassure her. To show her that she had no reason to be ashamed. Paige might be a few years older, but it had become obvious that I was the more experienced of us two.

"I don't give a shit about that." I turned her face toward mine and pressed a kiss to her lips. Her eyes were drunk with lust. I moved down the bed, tugging the sheet with me, until I was eye level with those playful panties.

I pressed my nose against the juncture between her thighs and inhaled sharply. Her scent made my mouth water and my cock throb. "Fuck, you smell good, princess."

She let out a soft groan. Her hips twitched up, reflexively seeking more.

Deciding I needed a lot more than just her moans, I sat up and placed one hand on the column of her throat, stroking the hollow there and meeting her wide gaze. I needed to know what she was thinking. "When I fuck you with my tongue, there will be no holding back from either of us."

Her pupils were dilated and her lips parted. She looked beautiful like this, vulnerable and very much turned on, and I hadn't even done anything yet other than accidentally flash her the tip of my cock.

"I want you to tell me everything you're thinking, everything you're feeling. Do you understand?"

She gave me a quick nod.

I shook my head. "Use your words, beautiful."

"Yes. I understand."

"Good girl."

I lowered my head again and placed my mouth over her panties in a firm kiss. Tasting those donuts, just like I'd promised.

"Jesus, Cannon." She squirmed.

Planting my hands firmly on her hips, I held her in place. "You're not going anywhere, not until I get my fill."

She raised herself on one elbow, her eyes wide,

almost frightened.

I mouthed over her panties, letting her feel the heat of my breath, but nothing more. It wasn't what she needed, and she let me know by whining in frustration.

"Lift up," I murmured.

She raised her hips. I slowly slid her panties down over her hips, her thighs, letting my fingertips trail over the curve of her calves as I went. When my eyes met tender pink flesh, I sucked in a breath.

"You have a beautiful vagina." I parted her with my thumb, stroking softly. Her lips were already plump and flushed, glistening wet with arousal. My mouth watered with desire. I was so hungry to taste her—but I had to be patient. I had to make her tell me what she wanted.

She pressed her palms over her eyes. "Oh my God, did you just say that?"

I brushed my lips against her center, leaving a chaste kiss—well, as chaste as a kiss there could be. In my line of work, I had seen a lot of women who were uncomfortable even saying the words for their own body parts. But they shouldn't be. Especially not Paige.

"Yes, and I meant it. A perfectly plump little clit, cute pink labia, delicious scent." I kissed her again, this time letting my tongue slide over her swollen bud.

She sucked in a sharp breath and squirmed at my attention.

"Tell me what you feel," I said, barely pausing long enough to get the words out. Then I was right back to licking her.

"So good. Incredible," she said on a moan.

"You like my tongue against your clit?" I offered, enjoying her discomfort at having to speak the words.

"Y-yes!" she shouted as I sucked the bundle of flesh between my lips.

I alternated my movements, discovering what she liked. Spurred on by her shouts and moans, I nibbled and licked and sucked until she was bucking against my face. I whispered dirty words against her silken flesh, left bite marks on her inner thighs, and pushed her further than I suspected she'd been pushed before.

"Tell me what you like," I said.

"Your mouth . . . it feels so good. Right there."

Using broad strokes, I flattened my tongue against her, moving in a dizzying rhythm as her cries of pleasure grew louder. And then she was coming apart, pushing her hands into my hair and riding my face. It was a beautiful moment that seemed to last and last; each time I thought she was through, another low moan of ecstasy pushed past her lips and her body gave another tremble. Several moments later, when I slid up beside her, Paige was still gasping for breath, covering her face with one hand.

"Don't hide from me." I took her hand and kissed the back of it before placing it on my cock.

"Cannon . . ." She moaned, curling her hand around me.

All the pent-up lust and attraction from the past week crashed through me at once. "I need you," I hissed as she continued stroking me in long pulls.

"Yes." She rose to her knees, reaching for the bedside drawer. With trembling fingers, she produced an unopened box of condoms.

"Those won't fit, princess. I'll be right back." In ten seconds flat, I was back, sheathed in latex, and joined her on the bed. She'd stripped off her T-shirt, and for several moments, I just stared at her, took my fill of what I was sure was going to be a one-time lapse of judgment on her part. I still couldn't believe she was going to let me fuck her.

I lay back on the pillows, urging Paige into my lap. I held the base of my dick with one hand and guided her closer with the other. And then it was happening—the tight clench of her muscles around me, a sigh of pleasure pushing past her lips, and blissfully, no one to interrupt us.

"That's it, nice and slow." I bit down, my jaw ticking as she slowly—painfully slowly—lowered herself onto my cock. She seemed determined to take me to the hilt.

Finally, with a low whimper, I bottomed out inside her. *Fuck.*

"Christ, Paige." Her body fit me like a tight glove,

and I was unprepared for how right and perfect she felt. Her hair fell around us in a silken curtain as I brought her mouth down to mine again.

She was so needy and responsive, matching my thrusts and creating a rhythm of her own. Watching her was like viewing my own private erotic show. Her head dropped back between her shoulders, thrusting her breasts out for my waiting hands.

When Paige had called me out—suggested we sleep together to prove her point—of course I'd been game. But I'd had no idea it would be like *this*. I thought it would be like placing a checkmark in a box, a shot at living out my teenage fantasy.

But with her warm, pliable body writhing above mine, pushing her hips down harder and faster, her fingers clutching my skin, her soft, broken voice pleading for more—it was so much more than that. It was as if her every response to me was magnified, and I was watching it through a lens. My heart beat heavy and loud, my blood pumping hot and fast. I never wanted this to stop. And it was going to end way too soon if I didn't slow us down.

I remembered that she'd said it had been a while, and I wanted to make sure this was good for her. Placing my hands on her hips, I eased her pace. "Come here, beautiful."

She climbed down with a pout, like a princess booted from her throne, but she lay down on the bed where I directed her.

"We're just getting started," I reassured her, pressing a kiss to her full mouth. For a moment I worried if kissing her was too much, too intimate. But right then, I didn't care.

Paige closed her eyes and kissed me back, a sweet sigh on her lips.

Chapter Seventeen

Paige

Cannon was kissing me. Deep, drugging kisses that made my toes curl.

But then he pressed into me again, pushing my thighs apart, gripping my hips and plunging forward, and I forgot about everything else. The sensation of him entering me was unlike anything else. And the look of determined concentration on his face, like he was almost in pain with how good it felt? I understood that exactly. It was almost too much to bear.

His every movement was controlled, each one designed to bring me maximum pleasure. I never wanted this to end.

"Has anyone ever fucked you like this?"

"No. Never." That was the honest truth. He was so deep and so possessive, so vocal, commanding my attention and demanding submission. It was like fitting a key into a locked box.

Watching his thick length spear me—part me, plunge deep inside and then withdraw, wet with our juices—was almost obscene. When he bottomed out, I ground my hips against his pelvis, lost to the sensation. Allie's little brother fucked like a porn star. That wasn't a piece of knowledge I'd ever recover from. *Shit!*

"This pussy is mine right now. Isn't it, princess?"

"Yes, yours."

The way he'd pushed me outside my comfort zone, taking charge and making me tell him every stray thought, feeling, and emotion running through my brain while he pleasured me . . . it was too much, and yet I wanted more.

"Say my name when we fuck."

"It's yours, Cannon."

He grunted something like praise against my neck and began pushing harder, faster, until we were both racing toward climax.

Fairly certain he would leave fingertip bruises on my hips, I pushed harder and faster against him, wanting to see those marks on my skin later. I wanted the physical reminder of what we'd done, if only to make sure I hadn't dreamed this.

And then I was coming, clenching around him, milking him with a shout. Cannon gave a growl near my throat, his ass muscles tightening under my hands as he buried himself deeper than ever. I felt every hard throb of his cock as he pulsed inside me. It seemed to go on forever as waves of ecstasy rushed through me.

He kissed my neck, taking his time to pull out slowly and then roll over to lie beside me.

"Fuck, princess." He was breathing hard, his chest rising and falling fast.

A smile uncurled on my lips, and a sense of pride washed over me. The moment it was over, I knew that I'd won. Amazing orgasm? *Check*. But my feelings for Cannon? They were largely unchanged. This wasn't love. Thank God. That was the last complication I needed in my life.

He pulled me close, our naked bodies at ease together.

Cannon tugged the sheet up around us, and I rested my head against his chest. "Not in love with me yet, are you?" he asked with a smirk.

"Not even close." I propped up on one elbow, looking down on him. "You were right about two things, though."

He met my gaze with a soft smile. "And what was that?"

"You weren't kidding about your size or your stamina. But no, this isn't love. That was carnal lust."

"Agreed. Now, come here."

"But you said once. That was the agreement." *Any more than that could be dangerous for my heart.*

"You're not in love yet." Cannon's hand drifted under the sheet, sliding down my belly to softly stroke between my legs. "And this pussy is still soft and wet for me."

"I don't know," I whined.

"That was so fucking good," he said, turning toward me and kissing my neck again. "I want more."

"Just good?" I teased.

He slipped one long finger inside me. "Forgive me. Good was the wrong word. Incredible. Amazing." He withdrew his finger and pressed in slowly again. "So warm and snug. I want to live in there."

Cannon removed the spent condom and sheathed himself in another as I lay there, my thighs parted, ready for everything he could give me.

• • •

It had been two days since we'd had sex, and life had moved on. I went back to work, and so had Cannon, and we acted like everything was normal. He gave no indication that his world had been knocked off its axis, so of course I'd done what I needed to do to convince him we were cool. But today, things downstairs had taken a drastic turn, and I could no longer pretend I was fine.

My lady parts burned. They were swollen and angry and red. I knew exactly what was going on. God was punishing me for sleeping with my best friend's brother.

"Paige?" Cannon asked, rounding the corner

toward my bedroom.

After work, I'd collapsed on my bed and hadn't moved since. Cannon stood at my door in his scrubs, navy blue and faded. He looked so delicious like that; I didn't think I'd ever tire of seeing him dressed for work.

"Hi," I offered weakly.

A look of concern crossed his features. "What's going on?"

Pulling a deep breath into my lungs, I steeled my nerves. This was not a conversation I wanted to have. Ever. But it needed to be done.

I released a heavy sigh and met his eyes. "I think you gave me an infection."

His eyebrows pushed together, and he took several steps closer. "That's not possible. I'm clean; I promise. And besides, we used a condom."

We had used a condom. Both times that morning we'd made love. No, had sex. The L-word didn't enter this equation.

Cannon stalked closer. "What are your symptoms?"

Even though I knew his medical opinion would help, I looked away, stammering, "This is a total invasion of privacy." Picking at my thumbnail, I stared down at my hands. I prayed silently for the floor to open up and swallow me whole.

"Tell me, Paige. I can help."

My face was on fire. "It's red down there, and tender and sore. And itchy. I think I have a rash."

"Let me take a look."

My gaze snapped up to his. "No way. You're not looking at my hoo-ha."

"I already have, you realize. I had my entire face down there. If I take a look, I can determine whether it's anything to worry about. But I can't help unless I see."

I swallowed. *Fuck!* Of all the fucked-up situations to find myself in, I couldn't imagine a more embarrassing scenario. After sitting paralyzed for another few moments, I nodded and reluctantly stood to strip off my jeans.

Cannon went to the bathroom, and I heard the

water running. He was washing his hands. When he returned, I was standing beside the bed.

"The panties too," he murmured.

"Can't you just take a quick peek beneath them?"

He shook his head. "Take them off, and then lay back with your knees open."

Kill. Me. Now.

While I obeyed, Cannon's eyes traced my movements. This was just weird.

I lay back, propped up on pillows, and squeezed my eyes shut.

"Just relax, princess," he said, sitting down on my bed between my parted legs.

Certain I was going to die of embarrassment, I stared blankly up at the ceiling.

"Take a deep breath and open your knees."

Taking a deep breath to steady myself, I did as he asked.

"Interesting . . ." He hesitated, using one finger to softly touch my swollen flesh. His touch was so careful, so reverent, it made my heart swell despite my embarrassment.

"What do you mean, *interesting*? What the hell is it?"

He met my eyes. "How long after sex did the symptoms start?"

"I noticed it when I woke up the next morning."

He nodded. "That's what I figured. It's a latex allergy."

I sat up so I could stare incredulously at him. "I'm not allergic to latex."

"Your vagina begs to differ. We can develop new allergies over time. You'll be fine . . . you just need to abstain from sex until it's healed, probably three to five days, and then find a latex-free condom alternative going forward."

"Right. Well, thanks." I rose and tugged my underwear back on. I guessed having a roommate who was also a doctor had its perks.

"Are you sure you're okay? I feel bad. I was basically the reason this happened."

His sentiment was sweet, and yeah, in a weird way, his latex-covered schlong was to blame, but I couldn't fault him. A good time was had by all.

"I'll be fine." I shifted, wincing in discomfort.

Cannon frowned. "That's what I thought." He piled up some pillows behind me. "Lay back down."

When I resisted, frowning at him, Cannon merely chuckled. "You're not a very good patient. Just chill for a minute and let me make a phone call. I can't prescribe drugs yet, but I'm betting that when I call Dr. Haslett—"

"Who?"

"The attending physician I worked with in gynecology. I'm sure he'll write you a prescription. An oral steroid will clear this up fast. You'll feel better very soon, princess."

At his deep, silky voice not only promising to make me better, but calling me by that endearing nickname, I couldn't help but smile at him like a lovesick little fool.

I relaxed against the pillows while Cannon pulled his phone from his pocket and walked out into the hall to place his call.

A few minutes later he was back, looking annoyed.

"What did he say?" I asked. "Can I get the steroid?"

Cannon grunted something that sounded a lot like *yeah* and sat down on the edge of my bed.

"Then what's wrong?"

He shook his head. "The bastard wanted me to take a picture and text it to him."

"Of my vagina?" I shrieked.

Cannon's nostrils flared and he nodded once.

"Ew. That can't be ethical."

"I asked him to treat you without actually seeing you, but yeah, that's just creepy. Ethical or not, I told him to fuck off." He pressed his lips tight, still pissed. "He saw the light pretty damn quick."

A surge of pride, knowing Cannon had defended my wounded vagina's honor, coursed through me.

His expression softened to return my smile. "What do you want to do tonight?"

I blinked at him, sure that he wasn't implying we spend it together. I'd been operating under the impression that we were trying to keep our polite distance, making sure that, aside from our one-time affair, real feelings didn't develop.

"I'm thinking pajamas, carryout, and movies. You in?"

"Only if you promise to actually wear pajamas this time." I remembered the night he crawled into bed with me; he'd slept only in his boxers. And then, of course, what followed when we woke up was the reason I was lying here sore and on the outs.

"Where's the fun in that?" He smirked.

I wagged my finger at him. "Oh no, you don't. Don't be cute and flirty when my vagina's out of commission."

"You think I'm cute."

It wasn't a question, and I didn't answer. He was more than cute, he was damn sexy, and he knew it. Instead I just huffed, "I get to pick the carryout."

"Deal. You pick out what you want, and I'll run out and get it. I'll grab your prescription from the hospital pharmacy on the way." He offered me his hand and I took it, rising from the bed to follow him to the living room.

We ate Thai food together on the couch. Downloaded a Vince Vaughn movie that made us crack up with laughter.

"So, seriously, should I be offended that you're not in love with me yet? Maybe I've lost my touch," Cannon said, watching me with a challenging smile.

I chuckled, almost nervously, and shook my head. "Sounds to me like you're fishing for compliments, mister."

He shrugged. "Not at all. I just want to know, in your professional opinion, that one day when I find the right girl and unleash all this on her, there won't be any disappointments."

His choice of wording was spot on. *Unleash* was right. Cannon was a force to be reckoned with. He could have his pick of any woman he wanted, but that wasn't what he was asking. He was obviously trying to get a rise out of me.

"I'm sure you'd make a shit boyfriend," I said around a mouthful of pad Thai.

"Hey, I take offense to that."

I gave him a knowing smirk.

"I'd be the kind of boyfriend who held your hair back while you blew me." His voice was sincere, but his words were crude.

"How darling of you."

Reaching out toward me, Cannon pinched my waist, tickling me.

"Hey!" I scooted farther away.

"So you really can't think of any redeeming qualities that might interest the fairer sex?" he asked.

I no longer knew if we were playing around or if he really wanted to know how I felt about him. Since I couldn't admit that yet, not even to myself, I stuck with playful, rolling my eyes.

"As if Allie would let you date."

"Allie has no say in this. Assuming I did want a relationship."

My world tipped sideways. "I'm not ready to have this conversation," I said, my voice shaking.

Cannon watched me for several heavy heartbeats, and I thought he was going to press me to answer. But he didn't.

I stood to clear our dishes and take a minute to just breathe in the privacy of my kitchen. When I returned to the living room, Cannon was holding Enchilada up, and was taking pictures.

"Did you just take a selfie with my dog?" I was a sucker for a man who was sweet to my dog.

"Maybe. Is that a problem?" He grinned at me, and just like that, our playful mood from earlier was back.

Chapter Eighteen

Cannon

I'd rather be at the gym right now, pumping out some of my sexual frustrations, but instead I'd come to check on my mother.

"Mom, are you sure that's a good idea?"

I stood staring at the built-in cabinet my mom was currently painting royal purple. Her living room was a clash of colors, like a rainbow had taken a shit in there. I didn't know how her husband, Bob, put up with it, but God bless him, he did. He nodded and smiled at all of Mom's crazy ideas, shaking his head and agreeing that it seemed like a great plan.

Bob was ten years older than my mom, and after my dad left, I was sure my mother would never love again. And then she met Bob, the owner of the auto shop where she took her car for repairs. He had been divorced for many years, and had no kids. Mom seemed to fill the void in his life, just as he did hers.

"I love purple; of course it's a good idea. Everyone deserves to be happy in their living space, Cannon."

My gaze drifted from hers to the front window and the cloudless sky beyond. My living space was currently Paige's living space. The close quarters meant I was getting to know my childhood crush in ways I'd never imagined. I knew what she tasted like, how she moaned when I kissed her neck, and that she preferred almond milk in her coffee. I knew that before I came around, the most affection she got was from cuddling with her little dog. I knew she was a loyal, lifelong friend to my sister, and that she was totally off-limits.

It had been a week since we'd slept together. Five days since I'd diagnosed her with an allergy to latex. That evening we'd hung out in the living room, sharing takeout from paper cartons and reminiscing about long-forgotten childhood memories, laughing at the ridiculous reality-TV dating show that played in the background.

Thankfully, she wasn't mad at me for her predicament. Not that it was truly my fault. I'd tried to keep us safe by using a condom, and I certainly never intended her harm.

My mom crossed the room toward where I stood, wiping her hands on her coveralls as she approached. "I love you, Cannon-ball." She lifted on her toes and pressed a quick kiss to my cheek.

"Love you too, Mom."

It might not look like much from an outside perspective, but even me stopping by for fifteen minutes to check on her meant a lot. Bob worked long hours as a business owner, and I knew Mom got lonely. She and I had always shared a special connection. Despite my humble upbringing and the struggles we'd been through, she never stopped pushing me, never stopped believing that I could be more. Somewhere along the way, I began to believe it. I owed her everything.

Checking my watch, I saw my lunch break was almost over. "I have to get back to the hospital."

She nodded, then patted my shoulder. "Come by for dinner on Sunday. I'll make your favorite."

I didn't have it in me to tell her that meat loaf

hadn't been my favorite since I was twelve, or that her version was like a heart attack waiting to happen. I simply nodded.

"See you then."

Shrugging into my jacket, I headed out of the tidy and eccentric brick one-story she shared with Bob, and into the crisp autumn air.

Chapter Nineteen

Paige

I should have felt embarrassed being around Cannon now. He'd seen me at my worst, and while it had sucked, he'd handled it so professionally that I barely gave it a second thought. And he'd been right. Once I got on the medication, things cleared up quickly, and I was now as good as new.

Cannon had been so sweet and attentive all week long that I almost didn't want to burst his illusion that I was still under the weather. We hadn't spoken of it, which was fine by me. I didn't think there was a non-awkward way to say, "My vagina's all better now." So it was best to not say anything at all.

We'd eaten dinner together every night, each of us taking turns at the cooking, and he cleaned up the kitchen while I walked Enchilada. We fell into an easy rhythm, watching TV together at night until bedtime, when we hugged and went our separate ways.

But tonight, I wasn't tired. It was half past ten

when we'd gone to bed, and I'd been lying here awake for an hour. I knew a cup of warm milk would help me sleep, but I didn't want milk. I wanted Cannon. Wanted to feel the way only he could make me feel.

Emboldened, I rose from my bed and tiptoed down the hall. Enchilada followed me.

Cannon was obviously asleep under the blankets, lying on his side. His breathing was deep and even. I lifted the blanket, crawling in behind him.

"Paige?" he asked, his deep voice laced with sleep. He rolled to his back and looked at me.

"I had a bad dream." It was a lie. I was horny. And I was hoping he was too.

He opened his arms and I nestled in beside him, laying my head on his chest and hooking one leg over his waist. His heart beat steady and loud under my ear, and his male scent surrounded me.

Cannon released a heavy sigh, petting my hair back from my face. "I've got you now. You're safe."

"Thank you," I whispered into the darkness.

I let one hand wander beneath the blankets to rest on his stomach, and felt his abs tense under my touch. With my own heart thumping wildly, blood thundered in my ears. I knew what I wanted, knew I needed to make the first move, but the fear of rejection was a big and real thing. Cannon could say no, and if he did, I would be crushed. And not just because I was horny, but because I craved the kind of physical intimacy we'd shared last weekend.

Drawing a deep breath to steady my nerves, I let my hand drift lower. I could feel the waistband of his shorts, and my fingers slipped beneath it before pausing. Cannon's lungs expanded under my head, and a strained breath pushed past his lips. Neither of us said a word, and my fingers dipped lower until I found his cock, which was already at half-mast.

"Are you sure about this?" he asked.

"Only if you want me too."

"I'd have to be fucking insane not to want you. You're perfect, princess."

"Good, then we're in agreement." I crawled on top

of him, straddling him, and watched his lips form into a smile.

"And you're feeling better?" he asked with a grunt when my soft center made contact with his cock, which was now firm.

"One hundred percent."

I rocked my hips over the firm ridge in his shorts, swallowing a groan. This earned another mouthwatering grunt from him, and his hands found my waist.

"Christ, Paige."

His hands moved under my T-shirt, palming the weight of my breasts. His face was a mask of concentration in the darkness, and I felt bold and wicked and oh-so-tempting. I pulled my T-shirt off over my head, tossing it beside the bed, and watched as his gaze dropped to my breasts as if they'd been pulled by a magnet.

He fondled and caressed and squeezed while I writhed on top of him. I didn't even need foreplay tonight. I'd come in here ready, but of course Cannon didn't know that. And even if he suspected it, he wasn't going to skimp on treating me right.

I worked my hips over his erection, the warm friction dizzying at how good it felt.

Cannon rose up on his elbows to take one of my breasts in his mouth, pulling a cry from my lips.

"What about protection? I'm not putting on another condom," he murmured against my throat between kisses.

The thought of having him bare, all eight of those thick, delicious inches throbbing inside me with no barrier between us, had me clenching.

"I'm safe. On the pill," I managed between ragged breaths.

"I think you just became my dream woman. I've never done that before."

Seriously? He'd never done it without a condom? I guessed it made sense. The ultra-responsible Cannon had always made safe choices. I was happy to be his first in that regard.

Unable to wait even a second longer, I rose up on

my knees, just enough to tug my flimsy lace panties to the side. Cannon followed suit, pushing the pair of athletic shorts he wore down low on his hips. His big, gorgeous cock sprang free. I knew calling a cock gorgeous was weird, but his really was. Veined and heavy, and shiny at the tip.

I took him in my hand, guiding him as I lowered my hips.

"You sure about this, Paige?" He groaned as the broad head of him met my slick flesh.

"Very." I lowered myself another inch.

"Then ride that big dick, princess."

Lowering myself all the way, I parted my lips in a silent moan. He'd filled me to the brim and then some. I couldn't move, couldn't speak, couldn't think. The most intense feeling washed through me, and I'd never felt more connected to another person before. I might not have fallen in love with Cannon after the first time we had sex, but real feelings were developing, and the tight feeling inside my chest when his dark emerald-colored eyes latched onto mine wasn't something I could explain.

He didn't wait for me to begin; he simply planted his hands on my hips and began lifting and lowering me, pumping into me like I was his sex toy. Watching his biceps flex in the moonlight, seeing the sheen of sweat dotting his forehead, his tensed abs, all of it was so erotic. The feel of him inside me was mind blowing. Every hard ridge of him was stroking me in all the right places, and within minutes our pace had me speeding toward release.

"Cannon, wait." I planted one hand firmly on his abs. I wanted this to last, didn't want it to end.

"Let it happen. Want to watch you come." He groaned, the sound tortured, broken.

There was no stopping it anyway. My climax ripped through me like a bomb had detonated inside my womb, my muscles clenching and spasming all at once in a cacophony of well-orchestrated bliss. Blinding light flashed before my eyes . . . so intense, a second there I thought I might black out.

"Just like that, baby." Cannon's fingertips pressed

into my skin, slowing my movements, making me feel every-fucking-thing.

It was heaven.

"Fuck," Cannon cursed under his breath. "You're squeezing me so tight. Not going to last . . ."

His grip on my hips tightened and his thrusts deepened.

I watched him like a fan watches a live performance—entranced and enthralled, unable to look away, even for a second. He was beauty.

"If you don't want me to come inside you, better climb off now, princess," he bit out.

I wasn't going anywhere. Placing both palms flat against his stomach, I rocked my hips back and forth, my ass bouncing on him hard and fast. Everything about this moment would be branded into my brain forever. The tick in his jaw; the deep, hoarse tone of his voice; the way he felt moving inside me.

He continued pumping into me as long, lazy spurts erupted from him like hot lava, marking me from the inside out.

When Cannon came, it wasn't with a shout or a moan, yet I would never forget the sound he made when he climaxed. His breath pushed past his lips in the softest, most satisfied exhale you could possibly imagine. So controlled, so masculine. It was the sexiest thing I'd ever heard. His release seemed to go on forever as hot jets of semen pumped into me.

"Jesus, princess." He lifted me off of him, pressing one soft kiss to my lips. He was still breathing hard, and so was I.

After I used the restroom—because, holy heck, condom-free sex was messy—I crawled back in beside him. Cannon buried his face against my neck, making me smile. We lay together for several minutes perfectly spooned, my back against his front. I ran my fingers over any skin I could find—down his thick forearm, along his large, lightly calloused hand, hands that would one day save lives. I couldn't believe how natural and comfortable I felt in his arms.

Cannon shifted and released a sigh. "This should probably be the last time, you know, just so things don't get blurry between us. You're my sister's friend. We can't possibly keep this up without getting discovered." His hand smoothed my hair back from my face. "And I would hate to complicate things between you and Allie."

I stilled, my heart thudding dully. I thought we were going to cuddle and drift off to sleep together. How wrong I'd been.

"Right. Of course." I wiped a stray tear away with the back of my hand, my throat tightening. His words made sense; of course they did. But in that moment, he was the realest, best, brightest thing in my world, and I hated that we would never be more.

But what had I expected? He'd told me from the onset we could never have anything beyond a one-night stand, and I'd agreed to it. Hell, I'd even been the aggressor, the one to coax him into it, wanting to prove to him that he could have an easy, casual relationship with a woman without her falling in love with him.

I wasn't even willing to *think* about the L-word, let alone speak it out loud. Cannon and I had lived together a couple of weeks, had sex a total of three times. People didn't fall in love that quickly, did they?

I rose from his bed, fixing my face in a neutral smile. "Good night."

His gaze lingered on my bare breasts, and for a moment I thought he might invite me back to bed, maybe for another round, or perhaps just to sleep beside him. Instead he groaned, his gaze jumping up to mine at long last.

"Night, princess."

I thought he might make some sultry remark like, "You better go before I change my mind." Or put his hand between my legs to coax me into a repeat. But he didn't. He tugged up the blankets around him and lay back against his pillows, a satisfied smile on his full lips.

I gulped in a deep inhale and grabbed my discarded clothes from the floor before making my way back to my own room. After pulling on my T-shirt, I collapsed onto my bed.

If only he weren't so brutally perfect—masculine, funny, intelligent, great at making fajitas, amazing in bed . . . the list went on. But most of all, he was right. He was right that we couldn't pursue a relationship. His sister would be dead set against us being together, and no man was worth sacrificing my oldest friendship. Not to mention the fact that us dating was totally unrealistic—he would be moving away soon, taking a residency at a hospital who-knows-where. I was certain he didn't want his sister's friend following him across the country merely because I'd gotten a taste of his cock and went all lovesick on him, just like he said I would. No, I had to be stronger than that.

And yet . . .

When he was away, I thought of nothing but him. And when he was home? My focus was unwillingly glued to him, tracking his movements through the house. Listening for any sounds from his room.

I had almost memorized the soft bluesy playlist he favored on his laptop, knew that his showers lasted exactly six minutes. I anticipated his routine like one of Pavlov's drooling dogs anticipated the sound of that bell. On days he wasn't working, he rose early and went to the gym, then he came home, showered, studied, and made something to eat. Sometimes he paid a visit to his mom or sister, and he liked to watch the evening news, occasionally with a glass of red wine. I learned he was interested in American politics and followed the stock market closely. I knew he was stressed over choosing his specialty and applying to residency programs.

I knew all these things, and yet, I didn't know the most important thing of all—how he felt about me. I yearned to know where we stood. Did our sleeping together mean as much to him as it did to me?

I curled into a ball under the blankets, my eyes open and staring blankly into the darkness.

• • •

"There's not something going on with you and Cannon, is there?" Allie asked, appraising me across the table.

We were enjoying a late breakfast at one of our favorite local spots. And while I might have been a little on edge around Allie, knowing that I was hiding something so major from her, I never thought in a million years she'd call me out on it.

Determined to act casual, I took a sip of my coffee. Inside, my heart was rioting. "No. Why?"

"Because if there was, I'd have to disown you both." Allie took a bite of her breakfast taco while I waited desperately for her to continue. "You know better than anyone how strongly I feel about my brother sticking to the path to success he's on," she said, wiping her mouth with her napkin. "We came from nothing, Paige. *Nothing.* And now he's going to be a doctor."

I set my mug on the table and took a breath. "I get that, Allie, I really do. But you have to realize that Cannon is a mature, responsible person. Living with him has shown me that. He's not going to throw away his chance at success for a relationship."

Allie sat up straighter in her seat. "He wouldn't throw it away, no, but if there was someone tying him down, he might make different decisions, might not accept an out-of-state residency at a prestigious program."

The food in my stomach might as well have been acid, considering how sick I suddenly felt. I should come clean right this instant. Confess my sins and beg for forgiveness. Instead, I tore my paper napkin into little strips, unable to keep still.

Did it even matter that I was hiding this from her? Last night he'd told me that would be our last time. No, wait. He'd suggested it should *probably* be our last time . . . there was a big difference.

Something inside me knew, despite what he'd said, this was not the end.

Chapter Twenty

Cannon

My shift on Monday came earlier than expected.
After Paige had sneaked into my room in the middle of
the night, the rest of the weekend paled in comparison.
She was so unexpected, so giving and responsive. Plus,
she had her shit together, a great career, her own place,
a level head. It was refreshing to be around a woman
who took care of herself. Most of the girls my age were
still trying to figure it out, still living off their mom and
dad, or looking for a guy to fill that void. Paige wasn't,
and that was sexy as hell.

I rushed through the fluorescent-lit hallway on my
way to the OR, ready for the busy day ahead of me. We
had an open-heart surgery this morning. It would be the
third bypass surgery I was assisting, and there was a
serious vibe, an awareness of the significance of our
task. Of course, the doctors and nurses were trained
well and had spent years preparing for these moments,
but that didn't mean they took it any less seriously than
it deserved. I was proud to be part of the team, excited

to be training to do these life-saving surgeries on my own one day.

"So, how's it going with you and Paige?" Peter asked, scrubbing himself thoroughly up to the elbow.

We'd been working different shifts, and I hadn't seen him in days. Peter's bright, easy smile instantly made me feel more at ease.

I stepped up to the stainless steel sink beside him and turned on the warm water. "Do I seriously need to explain this to you, dude?"

Peter motioned me with his hand, still damp with soap. "Please do. This ought to be amusing."

"When a man and woman like each other, sometimes they like to take off their pants and rub their private parts together."

Peter rolled his eyes. "You're asking for trouble, man. She's your sister's BFF. I'm pretty sure there's a rule against that."

I finished scrubbing my hands and dried them with a paper towel. "Whatever. She's hot. And cool. And when we're in bed . . . it's fucking magic."

Peter pursed his lips, his eyes narrowing. "Do you really see a future with her?"

My chest tightened as a foreign feeling washed over me. "Of course not."

He smiled at me knowingly. "Exactly. Then you need to stop fucking around with her. Let her move on and find her Mr. Right. You know even if they say they aren't looking for something serious, they are *always* looking for something serious."

Even if I didn't like Peter's words, I recognized that he had a point. Paige did sign up for that dating app after all, even went out on a date. The guy was a total douche, but still. Clearly, she was looking for more than I could give her. Maybe I was in the way of her happiness.

"Whatever, it's over. It doesn't matter anyway. We're done. That was the last time." I didn't want to talk about Paige this morning; I wanted to focus on the surgery that was about to take place.

Peter gave me a sly look that said *yeah, right.*

Dr. Ramirez brushed past us with a breezy good morning. He was leading the surgery this morning, and I always appreciated his no-nonsense, down-to-business style.

"Come on, let's get to work." I followed the doctor into the OR, my hands up and arms out in front of me, just like I'd been trained.

• • •

Four hours later, my entire world was turned upside down.

Every time we stepped into the OR came with risk, of course. But I'd been so certain that David Hancock—Dave, as he told us to call him, Caucasian male, age fifty-five, married father of three, soon-to-be grandfather of one—would be going home. Of course he would. We were going to make him good as new. Better than new.

One moment, things were going according to plan. In the next, it was utter chaos.

I would never forget the deafening silence in the room after all the machines were turned off and the tubes removed. I wouldn't forget the way Dr. Ramirez looked at me and said, "Get some lunch. It's been a long day." As if I could have stomached anything just then.

Instead I'd stumbled, wide-eyed and shocked, into the on-call room and called Paige. I'd intended to send her a text, but my hands were shaking so badly, I couldn't type. She must have heard it in my voice, because when I asked her to come to the hospital, she agreed without question. Thankfully there was no else in the room that contained a set of bunk beds, and I collapsed into the lower one.

Sometimes patients died, and I knew that as a doctor, I would have to live with that fact. I'd been trained in medical school to dehumanize the person I was treating and look only at the condition. I also knew from my training that there was never much time to grieve; there were many more patients who were also unwell and needed a sound-minded physician at the helm.

But in this moment, none of that mattered. I didn't care about my training, or the other patients who might need me. I could only think of the paralyzing stillness in that room, and if there was something different we could have done.

Fifteen minutes later, Paige texted me that she was here. I met her in the hall and guided her back to the on-call room, where I pulled her onto the bed with me. It was still warm when we lay down.

"Cannon? Are you okay?"

I closed my eyes and felt her fingertips brushing through my hair.

Locked in Paige's arms, I let out the breath I felt like I'd been holding since our patient took his last. If I thought it was hard to watch a patient pass over, nothing could have prepared me for when Dr. Ramirez and I brought his wife and daughter into the conference room and told them that Dave had suffered a stroke on the table and stopped breathing. Their agony gutted me, and the bloodcurdling screams from his wife as she collapsed to the floor were heart wrenching.

"I don't know if I can do this," I murmured.

"Did something happen?" Her voice was soft and

timid, as if she knew the answer already.

"Yeah," I said, my voice cracking. "We lost a patient today." Even saying it out loud was difficult.

Paige was quiet for a long time. Then she shifted in my arms, and I felt her breath on my neck. "Of course you can," she whispered. "You'll come back tomorrow, and the next day, and the next day. You'll save many, many more lives than you'll ever lose. You're a great man, Cannon Roth. The world needs more men like you."

It reminded me of what Dr. Ramirez had said as I left the OR.

"What do we do now?" I'd asked him.

"Go home. Tomorrow, we'll come back as better doctors."

I exhaled and tightened my hold around Paige. Maybe she was right; maybe I could come back tomorrow and try again. But for now, having her here, warm and solid in my arms, was the only thing my fragmented brain could focus on. It was enough.

Hell, it was everything.

Chapter Twenty-One

Paige

Watching Cannon suffer today had been agony. Watching him lie on the narrow bed, his body clutching at mine like I was the only thing that could ease the pain, it did something to me.

I'd stroked his hair and murmured encouraging things, but I had no idea if it helped. He wasn't afraid to make himself vulnerable, wasn't afraid to admit that he needed me. It was everything. But then an hour later, his pager had gone off and he rushed out to attend to a patient, saying he'd see me at home. He left without even a backward glance.

I couldn't imagine a job like his. I worked in an office where the worst thing that happened in my day was if the printer ran out of toner. He'd watched a man die today, and worse than that, he felt responsible. He had blood on his hands, literally. I didn't know what would happen next, didn't know how you bounced back from something like that. I knew over the course of

Cannon's career, of course he would face death. But your first? Maybe it changed you for good. Maybe he'd never be quite the man he was before. I wasn't sure, and it scared me.

Checking the clock on the stove again, I wondered what time he'd be home from work. Surely the trauma he'd experienced today allowed him a pass to skip out early. Though if I knew Cannon, he wouldn't take advantage like that. Hard work and loyalty ran through his veins. After stirring the pot of homemade chicken noodle soup for a final time, I set the ladle on a saucer and poured two short glasses of whiskey.

I had no idea what might happen between us tonight, and part of me was hoping for something deeper than just sex. As great as that was between us, I craved more of a connection. I'd never taken into account how difficult it would be to have a secret relationship and not be able to tell my best friend about it. I needed advice, needed someone to talk to, to vent to, but there was no way Allie could be that person.

The empty, hollow feeling taking up residence in my chest was foreign. I'd lived so many years alone and had been just fine. So to have someone here, and not just someone, but Cannon, who was big and masculine and smart and sexy and tempting? It was slightly maddening.

The front door opened with a click, and Enchilada went running toward it.

"Hey," Cannon offered when I stepped into the living room. He shrugged off his laptop bag and removed his shoes. His expression was neutral, and anyone else would never guess the traumatic day he'd just lived through.

"Hi." I handed him one of the glasses of whiskey. "I thought you could use one of these."

His mouth lifted in a slight smile and he accepted the glass, clinking it against mine. "Thank you. Fuck yes, I could."

He took a small sip as I watched him, checking for any lingering signs of trauma. His throat moved as he swallowed one small sip, then another. Outwardly, he didn't look as if he'd fallen apart today. He was as tall and commanding as ever. Gorgeous and perfect.

I took a sip of my own, letting the liquor warm a path in my chest, then said, "I made chicken noodle soup. My grandma's recipe."

He smiled warmly at me. "Thank you."

There was a reason it was called comfort food. I hoped it lived up to the name tonight and put Cannon's mind at ease.

"It's just about ready," I said, leading the way toward the kitchen.

"I'm going to take a shower first. Is that okay?"

"Of course. I'll just heat up a loaf of bread in the oven. Take your time."

I knew I shouldn't have turned and watched Cannon's tight ass flex as he moved down the hall, but damn, it was becoming increasingly difficult to live with a man I was so attracted to.

After he showered, we sat down at the table and ate. When I asked Cannon if he wanted to talk about today, he shook his head. So I bored him with stories of my work, and showed him pictures of Enchilada on my phone. After that, things fell back into our normal, easy rhythm. We did the dishes, watched TV, and then went our separate ways for bed. Despair bloomed in my chest as I crawled into bed alone.

The need to comfort Cannon, to be near him, to make sure he was okay was unbearable. But I wouldn't go to him, not tonight. Not unless he made it clear that he needed me. The last time I'd crept into his room, he'd given me what I came seeking, the hot sex I craved, but he'd also warned me that we shouldn't do it again. I wouldn't be that girl—the kind who had no self-control, no self-worth, someone who would drop her principles at the door and open her legs. No, thank you. I had to be able to live with myself when this was done.

Movement in my doorway momentarily startled me.

"Hey," Cannon said, stopping in the door frame.

"Is everything okay?" I sat up in bed, studying him in his gray sleep shorts that hung invitingly low on his hips.

"Yeah." He rubbed the back of his neck, looking

unsure like I'd never seen him before. "You okay with some company?"

And because I couldn't say no to one of Cannon's requests, even if I wanted to, I nodded. It was the first sign that maybe we weren't yet done, despite what he'd said.

Soon we were spooned together under the blankets.

"Thanks for today, Paige," he said, his voice low and sleepy.

"Of course." I didn't do much other than sneak out of work early to comfort a friend, but I was glad it had helped in some small way.

"It's crazy, but today opened my eyes to what I want to do, what I've always been interested in but didn't trust myself."

"What's that?"

"I want to be a cardiologist. I know it's competitive; I know it's going to be tough. I know over the course of my career, I'll have days like today that will make me wonder why I chose this at all, but something you said today really stuck with me."

"What did I say?"

"That I'd save many more lives than I would lose."

"It's true, you know," I whispered back.

"I know," he said, placing a tender kiss against my forehead.

He tugged me close so that I was nuzzled against his bare chest, smelling his intoxicating scent—bodywash and Cannon. He was opening up to me, in more ways than one, and I liked being there for him when he needed me.

Cannon whispered good night and tightened his grip around me once more.

I knew this couldn't last. Playing pretend with my best friend's little brother was one thing, but actually having a real relationship with him was quite another. But I also knew that I didn't want to pretend anymore.

Chapter Twenty-Two

Paige

The phone call that came in the middle of the night startled us both. I knew by now that Cannon slept with his cell next to the bed, and since he used it as his alarm clock, the volume was kept turned up.

When I woke up, he was yelling something into the phone.

"No. Fuck no!" he roared before punching one fist into the mattress. "Just breathe. I'll be right over."

"Cannon?" I sat up in bed, my heart pounding a million beats a minute. "Who was that?"

"My mom," he croaked, his voice still hoarse with sleep. "My stepdad's dead."

• • •

Bob's death sent a shock wave through the family. As expected, Cannon's mom was nearly inconsolable, but he and Allie weren't faring much better. In the years that their mom had been married to him, Bob had been her rock. He'd taken care of everything for Susanne, providing her with a nice home, a comfortable life, and most of all, love and stability. Now all of that had been ripped away, it wasn't easy watching Cannon and Allie have to face their mother's new reality.

Bob was Jewish, so after the formal funeral proceedings at the synagogue, we were now back at the house to sit shivah, which meant the mirrors in the house were covered and the lights were kept low, with candles burning instead. Bob's sister had come over to instruct Susanne since none of the Roth side of the family were Jewish, and they didn't know the correct procedures.

I was sitting at the kitchen island sipping a bottle of beer. I didn't even like beer, but Allie and I were hiding in the kitchen, and that was all that was available. Finger foods and a couple of bottles of wine were set out in the living room, but I didn't want to abandon Allie, and I definitely didn't want to get into another long conversation with one of Bob's relatives.

Bob had had a massive heart attack in his sleep.

Although he'd always been a snorer, Susanne had noticed he was unusually silent that night. And rather than revel in the silence and get a good night's sleep, she said she immediately knew something was wrong. It was just after midnight when she discovered her husband wasn't breathing. She'd called 911, and then while she waited for the ambulance to arrive, she'd called her son who was soon to be a doctor. He'd rushed right over.

After taking another long swig from my bottle, I gave Allie's shoulder an encouraging pat. "It'll be okay, somehow, Allie. It has to, right?"

She sniffed and gave me a slight nod. "Yeah. It will. I'm just worried about Cannon."

Cannon? What did he have to do with any of this?

"What do you mean?" I expected that she'd be worried about her mom. Or that she'd feel awful about Bob.

Allie pushed a chunk of chestnut-colored hair behind her ear. "Cannon has been taking care of our mom since he was a little boy. But when she met Bob and got married, Cannon could finally just be Cannon—

a normal college kid, focusing on his own goals and aspirations."

I frowned, knowing that was never actually true. I was fairly certain that Cannon's master plan in life was always to take care of his mom, regardless of whether Bob was in the picture or not. It was one of the reasons he chose a career path that would set him up financially to be able to help; it was just who he was. But I wasn't about to argue with Allie. Their entire family had been through enough these past forty-eight hours.

Cannon chose that exact moment to enter the kitchen. He looked tired. There were dark circles under his eyes, and his expression was etched into a scowl. Yet he still managed to look rugged and masculine and beautiful.

Ever since he'd left my bed in the middle of the night, he'd been staying here at his mom and Bob's house. Well, I supposed now it was just his mom's house. Part of me couldn't help but wonder if he'd decide to move in here with her now. It was a forty-five-minute drive to the hospital, instead of the ten-minute drive from my place, but I knew that if she needed him,

Cannon wouldn't hesitate. He'd pack his bags and wish me well, and that would be the end of my days with my roommate and the forbidden tryst we'd shared. It would kill me if he left, and I wasn't ready to face that just yet.

I was curious about how he was holding up, and though I'd seen him during the events of the last couple of days, I hadn't spent any time alone with him, hadn't spoken more than a dozen words to him. I didn't know how he was doing or what he might be thinking.

"Have a beer with us, Cannon," Allie said, patting the bar stool next to hers.

Cannon grabbed a bottle of beer from the fridge, and twisted off the cap before sinking down onto the stool.

We sat in silence for a few moments, each of us nursing our beverages and unsure what to say to fill the void. Life could change in an instant, and that harsh reality was sinking in hard for all of us.

Susanne poked her head into the kitchen. Her face was puffy and her eyes swollen, but for now at least, there were no tears. She was holding it together for the time being.

"Hey, guys, can I get some help with Bob's uncle Fritz? His car's stuck on the front lawn."

My eyebrows jumped. I'd met Uncle Fritz earlier. He was ninety-seven, and I was pretty sure he had no business driving.

Cannon rose from his seat but Allie patted his shoulder, forcing him back down. "Sit. Have a drink. I've got this."

I gave Allie a sympathetic smile and watched her follow her mom from the kitchen. I glanced over toward Cannon, searching for something to say. Without Allie sitting between us, we suddenly felt too close, too exposed. Like someone was going to walk in and take one look at us and know we'd been sleeping together these past few weeks. That was how real and palpable our connection felt. One look and someone would read every intense feeling, every secret desire I harbored for this man.

Cannon turned toward me, abandoning his beer on the counter. His gaze roamed over me, hungry and unashamed. A warm tingle spread over my skin as he wet his lower lip with his tongue, so brief, I barely noticed it.

"Come with me," he bit out.

His hand tightened around mine, tugging me along. Before I knew what I was doing, I was following him out the back door and into the dimly lit garage. It was quiet as all the voices inside the house faded into silence. Dust particles floated in the air in the swath of late-afternoon light pouring through the lone window.

We were alone for the first time in days, and Cannon didn't waste a minute. He kissed me roughly, pushing his hands into my hair and fusing his mouth to mine. I staggered a step back, confused and reeling from his sudden onslaught, but Cannon didn't let up, backing me up until my butt pressed against an old canvas-covered car.

I knew Bob had owned an auto repair shop, and I was sure this was one of his projects. It should have felt wrong to be here, using it as a prop in our depraved act, but strangely, it didn't. Bob was outgoing and sociable. He loved cars, but he loved his wife even more. I had a strange sense of peace knowing that perhaps he'd be happy this old car would still be of use. Weird, I know, but that was how I justified to myself what was happening.

When Cannon's hands skimmed up my thighs, under my skirt, I gasped into his mouth. "What are we doing?"

"I'm going to fuck you on the hood of this car, princess." His tone left no room for negotiation.

Holy shit.

His fingers crawled up my skin, evoking chill bumps as they moved north, hooking into the sides of my panties. I'd worn a long-sleeved, knee-length black sweater dress today. It had seemed modest when I'd put it on this morning, but now I could see that it gave Cannon the easy access he was craving.

Cannon tugged my panties down my thighs until they fell freely past my knees, stopping on my suede ankle boots. My brain was still scrambling to catch up.

What had changed from when Cannon told me we were done? What could he possibly be thinking when his mom and sister were on the other side of a door not twenty feet away from where we stood? What in the fuck was happening?

I pulled a deep breath into my lungs.

"Paige?" Cannon asked, suddenly stopping.

"Not like this," I murmured. "Not now. Not here."

His knitted brow betrayed his confusion. "You don't want this?"

Strange, considering he was the one who'd said we couldn't do this anymore.

Just then the door to the house opened and Allie stuck her head out, her gaze landing on us. Thank God my legs were hidden behind the car, and she couldn't see the panties resting at my feet. Thank God we weren't kissing when the door opened.

"What's going on?" she asked, taking a step out into the garage, her eyes narrowing as she appraised us.

Cannon's hand came to rest against my lower back, as if he sensed my rising level of panic. The small gesture was meant to calm me, to keep me in place and prevent me from freaking out.

"We were just getting some air. We'll be right in." His tone was sure and steady.

A moment of tense silence followed, and my heart thundered in my chest.

Then Allie's mouth lifted in an understanding smile. "Okay. See you in a minute."

The moment the door closed, I sucked in a deep breath. Cannon dropped to one knee in front of me, sliding my panties back up my legs and securing them in place.

"I'm sorry," he said simply as he rose to stand again before me.

I shook my head. "I said not here; I didn't say not ever." Part of me hated myself for caving, but the other part of me was giddy with the promise of having Cannon in my bed yet again.

He nodded once, looking almost relieved.

"Are you okay?" I asked. It had been a rocky couple of days, losing his first patient and then his stepfather, all within a matter of twenty-four hours.

Cannon stroked my cheek with his thumb. "I will be."

"We better get back inside."

He nodded and led the way to the door.

That was way too close a call. But nothing could have prepared me for what happened later.

Chapter Twenty-Three

Paige

After helping Allie and Susanne see all the guests out and clean up, we ordered a pizza, unable to stomach another casserole. The fridge was filled with the well-meaning intentions of friends and family, but we'd eaten nothing but broccoli-rice casserole and tuna noodle for two days straight. We needed a break, and as we sat huddled around the small round kitchen table, a large pie in front of us, a moment of calm settled around us.

"You all right, Mom?" Allie asked, wiping her hands on a paper towel.

Susanne nodded. "Yeah, sweetie. We'll get through somehow, right?" She squeezed her daughter's hand.

"We always do," Allie agreed.

"Where's Cannon?" Susanne asked. "He should eat while the food is still hot."

I hadn't seen him in hours—not since our encounter in the garage. For all I knew, he was avoiding me. Maybe he regretted how he'd acted; I wasn't sure. I focused on the warm slice of pizza in front of me and tried to forget the rest.

Allie nodded. "I'll go find him." She marched upstairs while Susanne and I continued eating in silence.

Susanne's doctor, a longtime friend of the family, had stopped by earlier with a package of antianxiety medication. It was a sample pack with only a few doses, and Susanne had taken one earlier with a glass of water. I knew it wasn't the answer long term, but was happy to see that she seemed a little calmer now. She was resilient and strong. I believed she would undoubtedly find a way through this nightmare.

When Allie came back, she announced that Cannon was drunk and would be down to eat later. It wasn't like him to drink heavily, and the pizza I'd just consumed sat like a stone in my stomach.

As far as him coming downstairs, I never got to see that happen. I cleaned up the kitchen and left about thirty minutes later for home.

• • •

It was just after midnight when I heard the key turn in the lock. Sleep had eluded me. Even though my body was tired, my mind had continued to race.

I sat upright in bed. Cannon was home.

My heart rate picked up speed as he moved around the house. When he kicked off his shoes at the front door and moved toward the hall, I followed the less-than-graceful sounds of his footsteps. Then there was a loud *thunk*, followed by him cursing under his breath. Maybe he'd stubbed his toe? I almost giggled, but then the shadow of his tall form was filling my door frame.

"Paige?" He wasn't quiet, clearly wasn't afraid of waking me. There was a rough edge of need to his voice, and it called to something inside me. My chest tightened violently.

Cannon blinked as if his eyes were adjusting to the darkness, then stepped inside my room. I expected him to ask to join me like he had the other night, when we'd fallen asleep, seeking solace in each other's arms. My first clue that this was not going to resemble that was when Cannon crossed the room and leaned over the foot of my bed, grasping my ankles to tug me down the bed.

"Paige." He said my name again, his voice breaking.

"Yes?" I whispered.

"I need you." The plea was so simple, and yet so visceral.

"Yes." I moaned as his hands slid up my bare legs.

I'd gone to bed dressed in an oversized T-shirt and a pair of panties. And in about three seconds flat, he had stripped me of those. Then his hot mouth fused over mine, kissing me deeply. He tasted of whiskey and desire.

"Are you drunk?" I asked, panting as I pulled away.

"Might be. Just a little. But not so much that I can't make you feel good."

He nuzzled against my neck, leaving wet kisses on my throat, and desire surged through me.

"That okay, princess?"

"Yes." I gasped, willing to agree to anything in that

moment. I just didn't want him to stop.

Cannon stripped out of his clothes, shedding them beside my bed, and then he moved over me, entering me with a soft sigh on his lips, muttering how perfect I felt.

Mixed emotions competed inside me. I wanted this, wanted him, but I wanted it to mean more than a quick midnight fuck to relieve stress. I wanted to wake up next to him, make breakfast together, kiss his perfect lips before I left for work, and share a glass of wine together in the evenings.

A tiny piece of me still held out hope, but most of me had resigned myself to the fact that I'd gotten myself into this situation—Cannon's secret fuck buddy. I wanted to be more than a warm, wet hole, and at the thought, I started to get angry. Angry that he'd shown up drunk looking for sex, angry at the lack of foreplay.

Cannon lifted my bent knee, tucking my leg up beside my ribs so he could get even closer, thrust deeper than ever before. This side of Cannon was new—he wasn't the gentle, attentive, playful lover whispering dirty things while he watched for my reactions. He was taking, pushing me further, fucking me harder.

"Are you going to come for me?" he whispered against my neck, his hips pummeling mine.

I buried my face against his throat and nodded.

"I love you, princess. Always have. Always will. I fought it for the longest time. But now that I've had you like this, I can't go back. Won't."

I sobbed against his throat as his hips continued bucking against mine. "Cannon . . ." My cry was ragged and broken.

Every bit of anger melted away. It was replaced by a love so bright, it blinded me to everything else. We'd figure this out. We had to.

• • •

A noise in the living room woke me, and since I could feel the weight of Cannon's hand resting across my waist, I knew he wasn't the one stirring.

Blinking open sleepy eyes against the harsh light outside, I reached over to nudge Cannon's shoulder and whispered, "I think Enchilada needs to go out."

He grunted something unintelligible, and I could only smile. I felt the exact same way, overtired and completely sated. We'd stayed up half of the night making love, and I didn't want to move. The first time was fast and rough, and I'd never forget Cannon whispering his love for me as he took me. The second time was slower, softer, and so meaningful. I had no idea what today held for us, but I knew we'd need to talk about what was going to happen next between us.

I stretched and noticed Enchilada lying beside the bed, still asleep. Then a voice in my living room called Cannon's name, and I bolted upright in the bed.

Footsteps drew closer. Someone was in my house, and they were headed down the hall.

I tugged the sheet up to cover my breasts as Allie appeared in the doorway.

"What the fuck is this?" she shrieked.

Cannon's eyes snapped open and he sat up in bed next to me, tugging the sheet up around his hips to conceal himself.

We had literally been caught red-handed. We were

naked and in bed together—it didn't get much worse than that.

Allie's hands were shaking as she brought her fingers to her lips. "No." She shook her head as if she wanted to wipe the image she was seeing from her brain. Her gaze locked on mine, and the hurt in her wild eyes was unlike any I'd ever seen. Her expression was more shocked and devastated than when she found out her fiancé was cheating on her.

"You're fucking my brother?" she managed, her voice breaking on the words.

My heart plummeted, and I felt sick to my stomach. I never meant to deceive my very best friend, but here I was, in bed with her brother. It felt like the worst betrayal.

"Al, give us a minute," Cannon said after a few seconds of tense silence. His voice was devoid of emotion, so unlike how he'd been last night, and my heart sank further.

Allie spun and stomped off down the hall. I was sure I had about thirty seconds to get dressed before she started throwing things in the living room. Lord knew I deserved every bit of her wrath. It wasn't just that I'd started seeing Cannon; it was the fact that I'd done it behind her back. Maybe if I'd been honest with her from the start, admitted my feelings for him and sought her blessing . . .

I tugged my panties up my legs and stepped into my jeans. Slipping my discarded shirt from last night on over my head, I smoothed my just-fucked hair back in a low ponytail. Cannon pulled on his jeans, going commando beneath them.

Not daring enough to meet Cannon's eyes, I held my breath and headed out, not ready to face Allie but unable to hide out in here with his stony silence.

"Hey." Cannon gripped my elbow, stopping me in the doorway. "Why don't you let me talk to her. Give her a chance to cool down."

I shook my head. "No, it's all right. I got myself into this mess, and it's my responsibility to deal with the consequences."

He nodded, his expression darkening. There was

some kind of wall between us, but rather than try to figure out what was happening between us, I headed out to find Allie.

She was sitting in the center of my couch with her hands balled into fists in her lap. My first thought was that she was angry, but when I looked at her face and saw the tears dampening her cheeks, I wasn't sure. She was obviously hurt too.

"Why, Paige? I don't understand."

I swallowed and lowered myself into the seat beside hers. "I am so, so sorry, Allie. It just happened."

Allie wiped her cheeks with the back of her hand. "So last night—that was the first time?"

I cleared my throat. "No. It started before . . ." Pretty much right after he moved in, which meant we'd been sleeping together for much longer than I wanted to admit to Allie.

"But you weren't even interested in dating. I tried so many times to get you out there more." Allie sniffed again.

God, this was painful. I couldn't tell her I'd fallen for her brother. Couldn't even admit that to myself, because I was ninety-nine percent sure things between us were now over.

"I'm so sorry, Allie," I offered again, my voice small as shame surged through me.

She hadn't stormed out yet, so at least she was willing to hear me out. I guessed after twenty-plus years of friendship, she wasn't going to just give up on me, as mad as she was, and there was some comfort in that.

"Can we please talk about this?" I asked. "Maybe go grab a cup of coffee?"

At least that would spare us the awkward moment when Cannon finally dressed and came out to join us. I didn't think I was up for having to face him this morning too. Allie didn't know it, but uncertainty swirled inside me over Cannon's middle-of-the-night declaration.

The harsh light of day revealed the truth. Cannon had been drunk. It was the only explanation that made sense. He'd been through two tragedies in two days, losing his first patient and then his stepdad. He was out of his mind with grief, and he was intoxicated.

People said things like that when they'd been drinking. The *I love you, man* commentary shared between boozed-up friends was almost cliché. That's all it was. I wanted to believe it was something more, but if he really was in love with me, he'd be out here right now dealing with the fallout, telling Allie that we were an item and not just a mistake.

He didn't love me. I was there for Cannon in his time of need, and he was appreciative. Not if he hadn't mentioned it today, especially not the way he'd looked at me when Allie was screaming. He looked like he wanted to get away from me as fast as he could.

Allie thought about my offer for coffee for a moment longer. I needed to get out of the house, whether she was coming with me or not. Finally, she nodded, and I grabbed my keys and phone before we headed out.

Once we were seated with two steaming mugs of coffee before us, Allie looked at me expectantly, waiting for me to say something. Only I had no idea what to say.

Admit that I cared for him? Where would that get
me? Maybe it was better to let her think it was a
moment of weakness, purely physical between us. Hell,
maybe it had been. The truth was, I had no idea what
was going on inside Cannon's head right now. I only
knew that he hadn't tried to come after me, hadn't told
Allie to get out and mind her own business.

"I can't tell you how sorry I am," I said,
apologizing again.

Allie shifted in her seat, crossing her legs as she
studied me. "How long exactly have you been sleeping
with my brother?"

"It started a little while ago. We're friends, and then
with us living together, it evolved into something
more."

"More as in . . . you care for him? You want him to
make sacrifices and stay behind now?"

I shook my head. "I care about him, yes, but I
would never make demands of him like that."

Allie let out a deep exhale, her grip tightening around her mug. "I have no idea what to say, Paige. I never imagined a scenario where you were hooking up with my little brother behind my back."

Embarrassment washed over me like a tidal wave. Unsure how to respond, I took a sip of hot coffee, burning the tip of my tongue. I was pretty sure that was karma.

I set down the mug in front of me. "What happens now?"

Allie's gaze drifted out the window of the coffee shop to where pedestrians and college kids were navigating our still-sleepy city. "Honestly? I'm not sure, Paige. Seeing you two in bed together isn't just something I can erase."

I nodded. This wasn't like the time I spilled marinara on her favorite white silk blouse. That was fixed with a visit to the dry cleaner's, and then we were good again. I had a feeling this would take a little while. I'd broken her trust. I couldn't just snap my fingers and make it all better.

"I need some time," she said. "And I still need to talk to Cannon. Find out what the fuck the little dipshit was thinking."

That made two of us.

Chapter Twenty-Four

Paige

Tears welled in my eyes, and I sank onto the couch as my legs gave out. Cannon had taken physical comfort from me in a time of stress. I'd wanted to prove his theory wrong and rack up a few orgasms in the process. We had both used each other. And now it was over.

But he'd crossed the line when he told me he loved me, made me believe he wanted to be with me. I was a quick lay, and that was all it was. Then why say all those things he could never take back? Why tell me he loved me? Those words on his lips had been the most beautiful thing I'd ever heard, everything I'd ever dreamed about, yet never hoped for.

My heart hurt. My body was sore from his rough, punishing thrusts. It was like there was no escaping, no forgetting even the smallest of details about last night. Except he'd forgotten the entire thing. He'd been drunk, I knew that, but I never imagined he'd forget such a crucial detail.

Losing Cannon before I ever really had him was the most painful thing in my small world.

Chapter Twenty-Five

Cannon

It had been a mere twenty-four hours since Allie had caught me with Paige.

That night had been perfect. After a grueling couple of days, I'd gone to Paige needing her sweet comfort. And it had felt so right, so amazing, that I couldn't hold my feelings inside any longer. I'd told her I loved her.

It wasn't something I had planned on telling her—fuck, it wasn't even something I'd planned on admitting to myself—yet there it was. And she'd merely clung to me, enjoying the pleasure I delivered, but not once voicing her own feelings. But what had I expected? This was never supposed to be about love. She'd ridden out the pleasure, milking me, loving me with her body but never with her words.

Christ, taking her bareback was an experience I'd ever forget. The way she'd sighed and softly moaned my name when I entered her, the tight grip of her body strangling my cock, the way her restless hips had thrust toward mine every time I slid back . . . she was perfection. And then Allie found us together and everything had turned to shit.

Allie was beyond pissed, and maybe I should have felt guilty about that, but Paige and I were grown-ups. We knew the score when we started this. Shit, Paige was practically the one who'd seduced me. Told me there was no way she'd fall in love with me.

I guess she was right.

The truth was I'd wanted her since I laid eyes on her when she answered the door that first day. I would never have acted on it, though, if she hadn't suggested we hook up. And if we'd never gone there, if I'd never gotten to hold her in the dark, never entered her tight, warm body, I wouldn't be so utterly messed up right now. She'd wrecked me.

It was easy to tell myself I was staying with my mom because she needed me, but the truth was my decision was motivated by the need to give Paige some space.

"Earth to Cannon." Peter waved his hand in front of my face.

Blinking, I looked up at him. We were halfway through a brutal twelve-hour night shift. Enjoying lunch at two in the morning would never seem natural to me. But at least I was sitting with Peter, who often brought levity to my life.

"You all right, buddy? You tuned out on me for a few minutes there."

I nodded and picked up my fork. "Fine."

Peter knew that I'd lost my stepdad last week. Bob had never felt like a dad to me, but he was a good man and he'd loved my mom, and that was good enough for me. His loss was devastating. Mom was cycling through the normal stages of grief, and I'd stayed with her every night just so she wasn't alone. It had actually been nice. We ate together when I was home, and she did my laundry just like in the old days. I think it gave her some sense of purpose.

Peter laughed, pushing his tray away. "Bullshit. You're not fine. And I'm not talking about losing Bob.

That was horrible and hard on the whole family, I get that, but this is something else."

Forcing down another bite of enchilada, I frowned. Enchiladas only made me think of Paige and her weird little dog. I wasn't ready to admit to anyone how much I missed them.

"Why don't you fill me in then, since you seem to think you know something I don't," I bit out.

"You're hung up on Paige. I can see it."

I raised my brows. This was not the conversation I expected to be having. "Not even close."

"You're falling for her. You speak fondly of her often, and you're spacey when you're here. It's happening. The great Cannon Roth has fallen."

Such bullshit . . .

Women threw themselves at me daily. Love was never even on my radar, and I had no plans to change that. My heart was like a steel trap, strong and certain. Sure, they could bounce on my cock for an hour, but saying good-bye was easy because my heart was never even on the table. My goals were singular, and I never pictured a woman by my side while I pursued them.

Period. End of story.

Until Paige . . .

I might have told her I was cursed when it came to sex, that women fell in love with me and then pursued me relentlessly after, but she'd proven me wrong. Paige wasn't in love, wasn't pursuing me. Shit, she hadn't even said anything when I admitted I loved her. Not even a thank-you.

It was a hard truth to face that Peter was right. I was the one who had fallen for her.

Finishing up in silence, Peter and I grabbed our trays from the table, stowing our dishes in the proper bins and throwing our trash away.

"Doesn't matter." I heaved out a sigh. "I've submitted my application for a residency."

"That's huge news." Peter grinned at me. "About damn time."

When Dr. Ramirez offered to refer me to a hospital

in Denver with a world-renowned cardiology program, I couldn't say no to that opportunity. Having his guidance and knowing he believed in me was everything. And with things the way they were with Paige and my sister, leaving town sounded pretty fucking awesome.

As we headed from the hospital cafeteria, a heaviness settled over my chest. Having selected my path, I should have felt lighter and at ease after all these long months of uncertainty.

Instead, the reality of my situation was hitting hard. I had fallen for someone I couldn't have, and now I was doing the only thing I could—flee.

Chapter Twenty-Six

Paige

A knock at the door surprised me. For a split second, I held out hope that maybe it was Cannon. Then I remembered he never knocked, aside from his first time. He had a key, not that he had used it in over a week.

When I opened the door, I was surprised to find a meek college-aged girl with soft blond curls and sad honey-colored eyes. She was petite, dressed in leggings and an oversized University of Michigan sweatshirt that hung from her frame and made her look even smaller.

She met my stare, seemingly just as curious about who I was. Then her gaze darted behind me and into the living room.

"Can I help you?" I asked.

"Is C-Cannon here?" she stuttered.

"Not right now."

"But he does live here?"

I swallowed, suddenly feeling uneasy, not to mention I was totally unsure about how to answer her question. "I'm sorry, who are you?"

Her expression changed, and she offered a shy smile. "Sorry. I'm Michelle. Cannon's girlfriend."

My eyes about fell out of my head. "His *what?*"

Her smile fell. "I mean, I was. Now, I don't know what I am. I haven't talked to him."

Several things clicked into place at once. She was the reason he suddenly needed a place to stay. He broke up with his girlfriend and needed a hideout. I'd been an easy escape from his reality. My throat tightened, and I gripped the doorway for support.

"He didn't mention you," I said.

Her smile fell away. "I'm not surprised. That's Cannon for you. Our history is . . . complicated."

He'd told me some of his complicated past with women, but now I wondered if he'd told me everything. Apparently not, because I had no idea who this woman standing on my porch was. He'd never mentioned the name Michelle.

"And you're his . . ." Michelle paused, clearly fishing for information.

"I'm his older sister's friend." *God, that sounded so lame.*

"Ah. That makes sense. I mean, I didn't think . . . never mind." She grinned at me, an almost giddy smile that revealed her age.

"The next time I see him, I'll tell him you stopped by."

She nodded. "Please do. And ask him to call me."

"I will."

Michelle retreated to the curb where her little red sedan was parked, and I watched as she climbed inside, took one last wistful look toward me, and then drove away.

Still rattled from Michelle's visit, I headed into my small kitchen to a depressing dinner for one.

Chapter Twenty-Seven

Cannon

I'd been staying with my mom for the past week and a half. Though Paige didn't say it, I no longer felt welcome at her place. I felt even worse, because it was basically my fault that Allie found us that morning. I'd left my mom's in the middle of the night without saying good-bye to anyone, shown up drunk at Paige's, and apparently forgotten to lock the door when I got home. And I was hung over, so I didn't hear Allie come in until she was practically in the doorway, watching us with judgmental eyes.

Allie was still pissed at me, but I knew in time she'd get over it. If she thought Paige was going to be a distraction from my career, she was wrong. Paige didn't want a future with me. At least, that's what I'd been led to believe.

"Hello? Mom?" I called out as I let myself inside.

I found her in the kitchen baking. Mom baked when she was stressed; it was kind of her thing. A plate of frosted pumpkin bars sat on the counter, and a pan of brownies was cooling on top of the stove. Mom was elbow deep in a mixing bowl, kneading what looked like biscuit dough. I eyed everything with apprehension.

"Cannon." She smiled when she saw me. "Glad you're here. Hand me that canister of flour."

I did as I was told, then sat down on the bar stool at the counter to watch her work. "How are you holding up?" I raised my brows at the counters, which were now piled high.

"What? They're for the church brunch this weekend."

I rolled my eyes. Baking was a much better alternative to lying in bed crying, but still she was my mom, and I was allowed to poke fun at her idiosyncrasies.

"So, talk to me about Denver," she said, dusting the countertop with more flour.

I'd called her the minute the opportunity was presented to me, wanting her input, although ultimately the decision was mine to make. But all that was before

Bob passed. Things were different now.

"Mom, I can't possibly leave you now. Not after everything that's happened."

I hadn't told her about Paige and me, and I'd made Allie promise not to either. Mom had enough to worry about. She didn't need to know about the drama still stewing between us. Allie had reluctantly agreed through text message, still refusing to speak to me much.

"Of course you can, and you will. I've always known this day was coming, and I've been preparing for it for a long time, Cannon."

I weighed her words, turning them over in my head. I had never put myself in her shoes, never considered what it was like to be a parent, to know your children would grow up and leave you one day. But she was right; it's something you always know is coming.

"I was fine when you went off to Yale, and I'll be fine now."

I opened my mouth to argue, but the heavy crease between her brows proved her point. My mom had lived alone most of her adult life. My dad wasn't in the picture very long before cutting out, and she'd made it just fine. All those years, she forged a life for herself, tugging two small kids behind her.

Mom turned out the ball of dough onto the floured countertop and began rolling it out with a large wooden rod.

I was grateful when she met Bob and fell in love. It wasn't fair that she'd only gotten to have him in her life a handful of years. But then again, I knew life wasn't fair. It was from her that I'd learned how to take the sourest, bitterest parts of life and turn them into something productive. It was time for my mom to make lemonade.

"Cannon, there's something else I want to ask you," Mom said.

"What is it?"

"Your roommate, Paige." She hesitated, smoothing her hands over the front of her apron.

My heart thudded dully in my chest. Had Allie said something? Watching Allie freak out that morning hadn't been easy. But Paige's indifferent response toward me afterward had been much worse.

"What about her?"

"I watched how you were with her during the funeral. You were attentive and sweet, and paired with the fact that I know you harbored a secret crush on her when you were young . . ." Mom stuck her hands into the ball of dough once again. "Call it mother's intuition, but I just got the sense that maybe there was something going on between you two. And then you suddenly left and hightailed it back here."

"Mom, I love you, but I'm not going to talk about my sex life with you."

She made a noise of agreement. "That confirms it then."

I rolled my eyes.

"Is it merely physical, Cannon? Part of me always wondered if you two would cross the line into more than just *friend* territory."

"I don't think Paige is interested in that, Mom. And besides, Allie would never go for it."

"You never know, Cannon-ball. Many things can be solved over a cup of coffee and some conversation."

I pressed the heel of my hand against my temple, feeling the stirrings of a headache. "Doesn't matter now, anyway. You're right about Denver. As long as you're okay, there's no reason for me to stay."

It was too good an opportunity to pass up. And if Mom insisted she didn't need me, there wasn't anything holding me here. Unless you counted a sister I wasn't on speaking terms with, and the woman I'd always desired who was honest from the start about what she wanted from me—a few mind-blowing orgasms and nothing more.

Mom nodded, a small smile on her lips. "I know you'll do the right thing. You always do."

I wasn't so sure about that.

Chapter Twenty-Eight

Paige

Thankful for Allie's second chance, I'd jumped at the opportunity to join her for a glass of wine tonight at a local bar. Her friendship was pretty much the only thing I had left.

We'd discussed her desire to start dating again after the disaster that was James, but when the topic turned to her brother, my heart began to pound. I wanted to feign mild disinterest for the sake of our mended friendship, but just hearing his name was like someone had struck a match inside my chest. I felt hot and anxious, desperate for more information, for news about how he was doing.

"I think he's going to be wrapping up at the hospital soon," she said, fiddling with her cocktail napkin.

"What are you saying? Does Cannon have an offer already?"

Allie's mouth lifted in a smile. "He does. He's going to be a resident at one of the best cardiology programs in the country."

Gripping the edge of my chair to keep from falling off, I held my breath while I waited for her to continue.

"He's moving to Denver. Didn't he tell you?"

That right there told me exactly where I ranked on Cannon's list of priorities. "He hasn't mentioned it." Because we hadn't spoken in two weeks.

Allie's eyes widened. "He's known for a couple of weeks. I thought for sure you knew."

I set my glass down with shaky hands, the bottom clinking against the table. The news felt like a knife had been thrust through my heart, piercing the most tender place I'd kept hidden away. Allie knew that we had been sleeping together, but she had no idea how deep my feelings ran, how crushed I was when he just walked away.

Allie focused on her cocktail, not letting on if she saw my reaction. "He's been busy. I'm sure he was going to tell you."

"He hasn't been by for his stuff or anything. He's been staying with your mom." Admitting that felt like I'd lost the very last piece of him.

Allie smirked. "That's probably for the best, don't you think?"

My world suddenly felt small and dark. It had been nice having someone to live with, even better than I'd expected. Cannon and I got along great, and once we threw great sex into the mix, it had started to feel like the total package. Then he went and ruined everything by telling me he loved me. And now he was leaving.

For weeks, the dilemma I'd thought I was facing was to choose between my friendship with Allie or pursuing more with Cannon. But now it seemed the decision had been taken out of my hands.

• • •

I hadn't realized how much I'd missed Cannon's sweet Post-it notes until one appeared on my front door a week later. I peeled it from the sun-faded door with tears in my eyes.

I need to talk to you. Are you free on Friday?

That was still two days away. Why did it feel like an eternity? I was sure that he was going to tell me about Denver.

After letting myself inside, I pulled out my phone and sent him a text.

PAIGE: *Yes, I'm free on Friday. Do you want to come over for dinner?*

He responded a few seconds later.

CANNON: *I have the day off. I'll bring groceries and meet you there.*

It was settled; I had a dinner date with Cannon in forty-eight hours. Now I just needed to figure out what

I was going to say to him.

• • •

You would have thought I had all the time in the world to plan what to say to Cannon when I saw him, but you'd be dead wrong. Somehow two days went by in a blur, and now it was Friday—time to face the music. Cannon had texted when I was leaving work to say he'd gotten to my place early and let himself inside.

When I arrived, I was surprised to see the front door was left open, not unlocked but actually standing ajar. I hurried inside, looking around to see if anything was out of place. The door to Cannon's room was shut. I imagined, given his long hours at the hospital, that he might be napping.

As I made my way down the hall, I smelled smoke and paused. Not sure what was going on, I knocked on Cannon's door. With no response after a few seconds, I pushed it open. A can of gasoline was at my feet, blocking the doorway, so I reached down and picked it up, setting it out of the way as my brain scrambled to make sense of what was going on.

A candle was burning just inches away. The edge of Cannon's blanket was smoking as the candle's flame licked at it. He was lying there asleep, unaware of his treacherous surroundings.

Confused, I bent down and grabbed a book of matches lying on the floor, then the candle with the intention of blowing it out, but it was already too late. Flames had caught the edge of his blanket, which was now smoldering, and clarity hit me at once.

Michelle had been back.

I screamed Cannon's name, my voice echoing in the small room.

Chapter Twenty-Nine

Cannon

After making our statements to the police, Paige and I were exhausted, both mentally and emotionally drained. She stuck close to me throughout the ordeal, and my protective nature, the need to keep her close, flared inside me. With her tucked close to my side, we surveyed her place. Thankfully, the damage was minimal. The fire had barely caught, only really ruining the blankets on my bed before Paige came home and found me passed out from lack of sleep.

She paced the living room, ringing her hands. I sensed that her home was the last place she wanted to be right now.

"Do you want to go out? Get something to eat?" I asked, running my hands up and down her arms. I hated that she'd been put through this. Hated my history and long list of unstable exes.

Paige nodded. Neither of us felt like cooking, but we were both hungry, it seemed.

I drove us to a nearby pizza place where we sat at a booth with paper plates of greasy pepperoni pie. It was about as far from a romantic first date as you could get.

"Are you okay?" I asked.

We'd barely spoken in the hours since she'd come home. The shock and potentially devastating consequences of what could have happened were weighing on us both. If I hadn't woken and the fire had spread, that gas can at the door would have ensured my demise. I didn't want to think about that, though.

When the police had asked if anything unusual had happened lately, Paige mentioned that Michelle had stopped by looking for me just a few days ago. Knowing that solidified in my mind exactly which of my exes must have done this. I gave the police a thorough description of Michelle including her car, where she lived, where she liked to hang out, everything. Allie had been right—I should have filed a restraining order back when Michelle broke into my apartment. I never imagined she'd up the ante like this.

"I guess you were right," Paige said, setting down her half-eaten slice and wiping her hands with a paper napkin.

"About what?"

"Being a god in bed and women falling in love with you." She looked down as she said this, and I wanted more than anything to see her eyes in that moment.

I wanted to believe she was talking about herself, but I knew she was talking about Michelle. "You broke the curse. Guess I should say thank you for that."

This time she looked up and her eyes met mine, but I hated what I saw in their depths. She looked so unhappy. I wanted more than anything to make that sadness go away, but all I could offer her was a smile. Paige returned the gesture, but her own smile was sad and didn't reach her eyes.

"I don't want to leave things weird and unfinished between us," I said.

"How are things supposed to be now, Cannon? I don't see you for two weeks, and then your psycho ex shows up out of nowhere. Allie's still pissed at me, and . . ."

When she paused and let out a shaky breath, I reached over and squeezed her hand. It had been a traumatic day, and I didn't want to push her.

"I'm just tired, Cannon."

I nodded. "Come on, I'll take you home."

Chapter Thirty

Paige

Days slipped past and I fell into despair. The moment I saw Cannon lying on the bed with the flames dancing so near, was when I knew for certain I loved him. A deep, aching love that wasn't going to go away.

I wished I'd been bold enough to tell him about that night he'd pledged his love for me. But what would it change between us? Yes, I loved him too with all my heart, but I wouldn't be the one to hold him back.

I hated myself for not confronting him the second I had the chance. I hated myself even more for searching for job openings in Denver on my lunch break at work. I knew things were over between us, but that didn't stop my brain from fantasizing about what it would be like to start over, to move to a new city, to explore things for real with Cannon.

On the outside, my life had gone back to normal. I worked, ate, slept, and went to the gym, but night after night, alone in my house, I cried myself to sleep. While I still had somewhat of a strained relationship with Allie, I felt sure over time our friendship would recover.

It was Friday evening, and Allie was over for an adult beverage and a marathon of our favorite show on Netflix about a pack of single women living it up in the city. It was almost comical how far the scenario was from our lives, but maybe that was why we liked it—it was a chance to escape reality for an evening.

I set a cranberry-vodka cocktail in front of Allie on the coffee table, and then sat down beside her with my own stiffer version. "Cheers."

She raised her glass to her lips. "Yummy. Thanks."

Pointing the remote at the TV, I hit PLAY on the show, our third episode of the night, and probably not our last.

"I want to say something to you, but I don't want you to take it the wrong way." She paused to adjust her skirt while I tried to figure out what was on her mind.

I set my cocktail down in front of me. "Just say it, Al."

She placed one hand on my shoulder and gave me a small smile. "Don't look back. If Cinderella had gone back for her shoe, she wouldn't be a princess today."

It was her way of telling me I needed to accept this and move on. I guess she knew, or at least suspected, that there were deeper feelings between Cannon and me than I was letting on. And the thing was, as much as it hurt, she was right. I needed to accept the way things turned out. I didn't say anything, wasn't sure if I was expected to, but I returned her smile.

"When's he moving?" I asked after a few minutes of silence between us. I wasn't sure if she was watching the show or merely staring blankly into space like I was.

"He leaves tomorrow," she said, squeezing the lime wedge in her drink and licking her fingers. She raised her glass to mine again. "On to bigger and better."

My eyes might have been on the screen, but I didn't see a thing. My entire being was focused on the fact that the man who'd stolen my heart was taking it with him when he moved halfway across the country tomorrow. And there wasn't a damn thing I could do about it.

Chapter Thirty-One

Paige

CANNON: I fly out this afternoon. Wasn't sure if you wanted to see me before I left.

Cannon's text message that morning came as a surprise. I was lying in bed thinking of him and my talk with Allie last night when my phone chirped, signaling a new message. I could only wonder if he was lying in bed across town thinking of me too.

After hearing nothing from him since the fire last week, I expected him to leave without a backward glance. Of course I wanted to see him, but when I thought about how that meeting would go, doubts began to creep in.

What would we say—I'll miss you? Have a good life? That was too painful to think about. I'd come to terms with the fact that I'd have to watch him move on from afar, that I'd occasionally hear updates from Allie. I was sure he'd be a brilliant doctor and have a beautiful life. And I knew one day he'd meet someone and marry.

PAIGE: *It's probably better if we don't.*

There was no reply after that.

But two hours later, I found myself Googling flight times to Denver. I hightailed my ass to the airport, hoping to see him before he left with a piece of me I'd never get back. I didn't care how bad it would hurt, how awkward or stilted the conversation might be. I wasn't going to miss my last chance at seeing him.

When I arrived at the airport, I navigated to the terminal I'd researched. There was a flight to Denver leaving in under two hours. If he wasn't on this flight, there was another taking off in about four hours. I had all day, and I would be patient.

I was only there five minutes when his mom's little silver sedan slipped past me in traffic. Ducking my head, I slid on my sunglasses, hoping no one spotted me.

I waited several car lengths away and watched as Allie and his mom dropped him off at the curb, hugging and kissing him like they were sending him off to war. Cannon was quiet, pensive, but didn't seem overly upset. I knew he was probably excited for this next phase of his life.

When his mom's car pulled away, I pushed my gearshift into park and hopped out, clutching the Post-it note I'd hastily written before I left.

Hoisting his duffel bag high on his shoulder, he pulled a massive black rolling suitcase behind him. I guessed he was having his other stuff shipped to his new home. Then again, he really didn't have much. The king-sized bed he'd bought was still sitting unused in my guest room. It was crazy how your entire life could be boiled down to fit inside two suitcases.

As my feet carried me up the sidewalk and closer toward him, my heart began to pound.

He reached the counter for curbside bag check and lifted his bags onto the conveyor with ease. I took a deep breath, now just fifteen feet behind him.

Sometimes there are no second chances. Sometimes it's now or never.

The attendant, a pretty young woman with a long blond ponytail, smiled at Cannon, and he smiled back. She made some joke that I couldn't hear, and Cannon broke out into laughter.

I stopped so abruptly, the man behind me almost ran into me. My feet wouldn't go any further. Cannon wasn't torn up; he wasn't heartbroken or distraught. He was smiling and laughing as he chatted with the bag attendant. He obviously never meant that *I love you*.

I wouldn't make a fool of myself, chasing after him like some lovesick little girl.

Crumpling the note in my hand, I turned around and headed for the safety of my car. The pain of losing him hurt all over again. As I drove away, tears freely streaming down my cheeks, I knew there wasn't enough chocolate or alcohol in the world to make the pain of this moment go away.

And the worst part was, I wouldn't even have my best friend to help me get through this.

Chapter Thirty-Two

Cannon

I'd been in Denver for two weeks, and every day I told myself today was the day I'd start feeling better. Today was the day I'd get over Paige and finally be okay.

The only saving grace was that I threw myself into my work. My days were busy and stressful, and I didn't have time to dwell on the past. But the persistent ache in my chest made it hard to forget her completely. It was a little too fucking ironic for me that my first weeks as a cardiologist were spent with a broken heart.

After a grueling twelve-hour shift, I was ready to go home. I pulled off my lab coat and stuffed it into my bag. Gathering up my stuff, I closed my locker and headed out. I still hadn't gotten used to walking out into the bright sunlight after a long night shift. The blackout curtains in my new apartment ensured I slept while the rest of the world was busy.

I fished my cell phone from my pocket and dialed my mom. It was mid-morning in Michigan, and I knew she'd be home.

"Morning," she sang when she answered.

"Hey, Mom."

"Just get off work?" she asked.

I fought back a yawn. "Yeah. How are you? Any plans for today?" Though I knew she was doing okay, it didn't stop me from checking in on her a few times a week.

"Not really. Allie and I might go shopping tonight. Did you decide to join that softball league?" she asked, referring to the doctor's softball league I'd been invited to join.

"Yeah, I think I'm going to." At least it would get me off my ass after work.

"Good." Mom sighed. "I don't like the idea of you being lonely."

"I'll be fine, Mom. Don't worry about me." I slipped into my car and started it, pulling out of the employee parking lot underneath the hospital.

"You know . . ." Mom hesitated for a few minutes, and I was so tired that I forgot what we were talking about. "There's something I want to tell you."

"What's that?"

"If there's one thing I learned with Bob's passing, it's that life is too short to spend it unhappy, Cannon-ball."

In my mind, I saw Paige. Saw her sleepy blue eyes, pictured her soft body curled beside mine. That familiar ache in my chest was back. I wasn't sure if Mom's message was about Paige or not, but that was where my brain immediately jumped.

It was time to take a chance. Otherwise, I'd live with regret for the rest of my life.

Chapter Thirty-Three

Paige

I'd done something foolish and reckless, and it was coming back to bite me in the ass. When I first learned that Cannon was moving to Denver, I'd sent off my résumé on the spur of the moment to a company looking to hire a human resources manager. It was a big firm in downtown Denver, and the pay was substantially better than I made now. At the time, I told myself it was a great opportunity, so why not just apply and see what happened?

Well, the recruiter had called me twice in the past week, leaving voice mails on my phone, and I was too much of a chicken shit to call her back. I hated the idea of being unprofessional and dodging her calls, especially when the opportunity was so great, but what was I supposed to do? Cannon might have taken my heart, but I wasn't going to give him my dignity too.

While I was trying to figure that out, something even bigger happened. It was Thursday night after work, and like usual, I took Enchilada outside and checked the mail. There was a letter with no return address, but the handwriting looked so familiar, the skin on the back of my neck started to tingle.

Without bothering to go inside, I ripped the envelope open right there on the curb. Inside was a plane ticket to Denver, Colorado, and a Post-it note that read:

If we don't try, we'll never know.

It wasn't exactly a declaration of love, but I wanted to jump for joy. Cannon wanted me there. He wanted to try. It was something.

With my heart galloping in my chest, the first thing I did when I got inside was to call Cannon.

"Are you sure about this?" I asked when he answered.

Cannon chuckled. "Hi, Paige."

The rich masculine tone of his voice shot through me like an arrow. God, I'd missed him.

"Hi." I was breathless, and I wasn't sure why.

"I take it you got the ticket?"

"Yes, but I don't understand. I thought you were moving on. No looking back." I sat down on the edge of the couch, stroking Enchilada's soft fur.

"Listen, I think I might have fucked some things up. After Bob died, and then Allie caught us together and freaked out . . ." He paused, releasing a heavy sigh. "I think it's better if we have this conversation in person."

"You want me to fly three hours so we can talk?"

"I'm hoping we'll do more than that." His voice dropped lower, and tiny chill bumps broke out over my entire body.

I didn't say anything because, holy hell, what was I supposed to say? My world was tipping sideways.

"Will you come?" he asked, his voice tentative and hopeful.

I suddenly realized how far he'd gone out on a limb by sending me this ticket.

"Yes," I said at last, my stomach tightening into a knot.

"Thank fuck. I missed you, princess."

Wiping away a stray tear, I looked down at the ticket in my hand. "I leave tomorrow."

"Yes. I'll pick you up at the airport at eight."

"See you then."

• • •

"Are you sure you're up for this?" I asked Allie as I handed her Enchilada's leash. "It's only for the weekend."

She gave me a knowing smirk. "It's fine."

When I told her about my surprise trip to Colorado, I thought Allie might freak out. Instead, she'd offered to dog-sit for me. It made me wonder if perhaps Cannon had told her about the ticket before he sent it. She didn't seem the least bit surprised.

"Thank you again. I'll be home Sunday night." I handed her the bag containing Enchilada's food dish, his favorite blanket, and a canister of his dog food.

"Don't worry about us. We'll be fine."

"Be good for Allie," I murmured, bending down to stroke his soft gray fur one last time.

"You doing all right?" she asked when I rose to my feet. Allie's brown eyes were filled with emotion, and the deeper meaning behind her concern hit me square in the chest.

She wasn't asking if I was okay leaving my dog for two nights. She was asking the question neither of us was brave enough to talk about.

"You gave me some really bad advice," I said softly.

"I know." She hung her head, looking down at her shoes briefly before meeting my gaze again. "I should have told you to follow your heart. I should have told you to run, not walk."

Tears welled in my eyes. Allie pulled me in for a

hug, her arms tightening around me.

I had my best friend's blessing at long last. The only thing left to do was go get my man and hope that nothing had changed between us in all these weeks apart.

Chapter Thirty-Four

Cannon

It was finally Friday, and Paige would be here in an hour. I felt like a scared teenager again, my stomach twisted into a knot, nervous over where the evening might take us and imagining it over and over. It was a little ridiculous how much I'd missed her. Since she called yesterday to say she was coming, I'd been wound tight, unable to think about anything else.

I spent the day vacuuming and cleaning my new apartment. I lived in a luxury building not far from downtown with a marble lobby and six floors. My apartment wasn't on the top floor but it was a corner unit, which meant I had two walls of windows that let in the afternoon sun, and a nice balcony.

After I finished tidying up, I headed to the grocery store to stock up for the weekend, since my goal was that we'd rarely leave the bed. I picked up wine and cheese and fruit for tonight, and ingredients for the French toast I wanted to make her in the morning.

Forty-eight hours with my princess wouldn't be enough. I just hoped I could convince her to stay long term.

I'd been with many women over the years, but no one like Paige. She was precious to me. Growing up with her, I watched her turn into a knockout beauty, never dreaming that I'd get a shot at something more with her. It was almost surreal to think that she was about to visit me here.

After showering, shaving, and applying a little cologne, there was nothing else to do but wait.

• • •

Finally, it was time to leave for the airport and wait for her flight to arrive. I got there way too early, of course, and the airport security patrol ushered me through the line, not letting me stop at the curb and wait for long. I circled the airport three times before she finally texted me that she had landed.

Paige looked even better than I'd remembered, wearing a light blue sweater dress, tights, and tall boots. Her honey-colored hair cascaded down over her shoulders, and she nervously tucked it behind her ear as she looked around. I realized she didn't even know which kind of vehicle I drove now, and in my excitement, I'd forgotten to tell her. I'd sold the old sedan that had gotten me through college, not thinking it could fare the long road trip, and now drove a black sport utility vehicle. Placing my SUV into park, I climbed out and called her name.

She turned at the sound of my voice, a smile on her lips. Dropping her overnight bag on the sidewalk, she ran into my waiting arms.

Lifting her off the ground, I held her close and breathed in her scent, so thankful that she was here. I didn't know a soul in this state, other than the people I worked with, and Paige's presence here felt like everything.

Chapter Thirty-Five

Paige

"How is it going? Do you like it here? Your new place? The hospital?" I wanted to know everything at once, and I was rambling like a lunatic.

Cannon chuckled and reached across the car's console to place his palm on my knee. He gave it a light squeeze. "Yeah, I like it a lot. I live in an apartment complex near the hospital where several residents live. The hospital was only built a few years ago, so it's new and really nice. And the cardiology team has all been very welcoming."

He made it sound like everything was peachy keen. I'd been barely holding it together, almost unable to get out of bed some mornings, and he was clearly thriving in his new city.

"That's good to hear," I managed.

Maybe he didn't want the same things as me. Maybe this weekend trip was just supposed to be zero-expectations fun. I couldn't allow myself to get my hopes up. Placing my steely wall up, I asked him about the landscape as we drove, and Cannon was all too happy to tell me about his new home, pointing out landmarks as we went.

I nodded as he spoke, sure that if I opened my mouth, I might say something I'd regret. I wanted to tell him that I missed him, that I was so glad I was here, but instead I stayed quiet.

When we arrived at his new place, he gave me the grand tour. It was a large one-bedroom apartment with walls of windows overlooking twinkling city lights. Inside, it was furnished with classy yet simple furniture—a tan leather sectional, long oak dining table flanked by two benches, and a bedroom with a four-poster bed and a two round side tables. It was nice.

After the tour, we stopped in the kitchen where Cannon poured us each a glass of wine. I couldn't help but notice the bottle—it was the same brand I always bought at home.

"That last night we were together . . ." he started, then stopped to clear his throat. He didn't have to clarify which night he was referring to. The night he came to me drunk in the middle of the night and told me he loved me.

My chest tightened at the memory. Taking a sip of my wine, I nodded again.

Cannon took my wineglass and set it on the counter with his. "I don't know what this is that's happening between us; I only know that I like it. And I don't want it to stop."

"You told me you loved me that night." Relieved that I'd been brave enough to finally get that off my chest, I inhaled deeply, waiting for his shock to come. Only it didn't.

"I know. And you didn't say anything in return. And then that morning when Allie found us, you rushed off without a backward glance."

Wait, what?

"You knew all along that you said it?"

He nodded.

"I figured it was a drunken mistake."

"Paige," he said, stroking my hand. "Nothing about us was a mistake."

I licked my lips, gathering my thoughts. I couldn't find the words just then to tell him that I loved him too.

"I have no idea what I'm doing," I admitted. Not a clue—with my life, with his beautiful younger man who should have been out of my league, not with any of it. I hadn't been in a real relationship in a long time.

His fingertips pressed against my lips. "It's my first time too."

He offered me a small smile, and relief flooded my chest.

"Come with me." Cannon took my hand and led me into the living room.

We sat together on the couch, my head on his shoulder and his hand in my hair. I'd missed the physical closeness of him so much that I wanted to soak in every moment—although I knew our conversation was far from over.

Lifting my hand to his mouth, Cannon placed a

chaste kiss against my palm. "I thought I should have been able to get over this, to move past it. That in time, my memories of you would fade. I thought I'd move on and do just like I'd been doing my entire life . . .

"Making lemonade," I said, finishing the sentence for him.

He took my hands in his. "Yes. Only that didn't happen. I missed you, Paige. More with each passing day."

"I missed you too." Summoning my courage, I met his eyes. "I'm in love with you, Cannon."

"God, I've been waiting to hear those words for so long, princess." He brought his mouth to mine, pressing a sweet kiss to my lips.

"Then why did you let me go so easily?" I asked, leaning into his touch.

"I didn't want you to compromise your friendship with Allie for me. And you're a grown woman, Paige. I figured you could decide what you wanted."

I nodded. His answer made sense. "And what is it

that you want?"

"You want to know what I want, princess?"

I gulped, nodding.

Suddenly he had me pinned beneath him on the couch, our wineglasses forgotten on the coffee table, the hard length of his body pressing into mine. I released a strangled groan when I felt the hard bulge of his manhood between my legs.

"I want you like this, every day for the rest of my life."

His words were so brutally honest that I could only choke out a shaky breath before pressing my lips to his.

Claiming my mouth with a searing kiss, Cannon rocked into me, both of us breathing raggedly. "Christ, you're so perfect for me, Paige. Say yes to this. To us."

Pulling back just a fraction, I met his soulful gaze. I saw all the love, devotion, and commitment I'd ever dreamed about.

"What's in it for me?" I asked playfully.

Cannon's gaze turned sinful and he leaned in to kiss me, showing me exactly what was in it for me.

He had me naked and writhing beneath him in about three seconds flat, but from there, he took his time loving me—on the couch, the kitchen counter, and then in the bed until I was a boneless heap.

Falling in love didn't feel like I thought it would— like I was losing a piece of myself to a man. No, it felt like I was gaining something else instead. Something bigger than just me. But I knew this something was so big and unpredictable that it had the power to completely destroy me if it went sideways.

For now, it seemed we had overcome our first hurdle. I just didn't know what would happen next.

Epilogue

Paige

As I shampooed and lathered and shaved and exfoliated, I thought of nothing but Cannon. Mindlessly going through the motions, I scrubbed every inch of skin under the hot spray of water until I was pink and boneless.

He'd spent a twelve-hour shift at the hospital, and I was missing him like crazy. Today marked my two-week anniversary of moving to Denver. I would start my new job on Monday, and while I was a little scared, I was also ready to stop mooching off of Cannon. I'd always worked, and so this felt foreign to me. I'd spent two weeks almost bouncing off the walls, ready to be productive. Cannon told me to relax and enjoy my time off, but I'd struggled with that concept and was glad it was almost over. I also missed Enchilada something fierce, but he was living with Susanne, and I knew she needed him and his sweet companionship more than I did.

Living with Cannon was an easy adjustment since we were already used to sharing a space. But this time it was even better. Instead of two separate bedrooms, we shared one room. We'd grown closer than ever these past few weeks, even making plans to travel abroad and do the humanitarian work we were both interested in. And last night, Cannon had even brought up the topic of weddings, asking which type I'd prefer, small and intimate or an all-out celebration. I could only imagine it was his way of hinting that a proposal might be coming soon, an idea I was totally on board with.

Stepping out of the shower, I saw his towel hanging neatly next to mine. Last night we'd cooked dinner together, and then he'd left for an all-night shift, kissing me softly on the mouth before he went.

Wrapped in a towel with a turban on my head, I grabbed a bottle of water from the kitchen, then sat down on the edge of our bed.

After blow-drying my hair and applying light makeup, I tidied up the apartment dressed only in my robe. I still had about twenty minutes before Cannon was due home.

As I rubbed coconut-scented lotion into my skin, I was suddenly struck by an idea. I quickly rummaged through the back of the closet until I found it—the sexy nurse costume I'd worn two years ago when Allie had talked me into that Halloween bar crawl. The night had been a disaster. Allie had run into an ex-flame from high school, and we'd hidden in the alley to avoid him. All the good this costume had done for me, escaping to the darkness for no one to see. We'd sipped our cocktails out of little plastic cups, cursing her ex's name, and then left a short time later. I wasn't even sure why I'd packed this in the move.

I slid the white thigh-high nylons up my legs, satisfaction blooming in my chest. Maybe this would give me the boost of confidence I needed to get out of my funk. I just prayed Cannon would play along. I added the inappropriately short white skirt that barely skimmed the top of my thighs and the matching top, which was so tight and low cut, it hugged every curve of my waist, forcing my breasts to spill out over the top. Then I faced the full-length mirror and smiled at my reflection.

Do I look silly or sexy? I couldn't tell.

The click of the front door opening hit me like a tidal wave, and panic rose in my chest.

"Paige?" Cannon called from the front hall.

The rich timbre of his voice sent me spiraling toward desire as I stepped through the doorway and stopped. He stood in the hallway, and his mouth dropped open when he saw me.

"Wanna play doctor?" I asked, using my most sultry tone.

Cannon didn't answer—just continued feasting his eyes over my skin, his expression growing darker.

The thin cotton scrubs he wore left little to the imagination, and as he became aroused by what he saw, his erection tented the front of his pants.

The situation was so playful, so silly, that with anyone else, I would have giggled. But not with this man. Cannon stalked toward me like a cheetah stalks a gazelle. He was all intense masculine energy, his gaze penetrating and possessive.

He took me in his arms, kissing me deeply. "Fuck,

you look hot," he groaned when he finally pulled away.

"Did you have a good day at work, handsome?" I smiled up at him, loving the way he looked in his scrubs, loving the way his strong hands settled on my waist. I loved everything about him.

"Let's just say I'm happy to be home."

I smiled again. *Home.* It really was. We'd built a home together, and it had all happened so fast. But all of our routines fell into place, all of our hopes and dreams aligned. All that was left to do was enjoy it.

I couldn't imagine a day would come where I wouldn't want this man with every fiber of my being. And no matter what life might throw at us, I knew without a doubt that together, we would always make lemonade.

Up Next in This Series

Smith Hamilton has it all—he's smart, good-looking, and loaded. But he remembers a time when he had nothing and no one, so he's not about to mess up, especially with his best friend's little sister. That means keeping Evie at arm's length . . . even though the once pesky little girl is now a buxom bombshell. A sexy blonde who pushes his self-control to the limit the night she crawls into bed with him.

Evie Reed knows she's blessed—with an exclusive education, a family who loves her, and a new job managing social media for her family's lingerie company. But she wants more, like a reason to wear the sexy lingerie herself. She has just the man in mind to help with that. She's crushed on Smith forever. Surely tricking her way into his bed will force him to see her in a new, adult way.

Except that when Evie's plan leads to disaster, she and Smith must decide—ignore the attraction sizzling between them, or become play mates and risk it all.

HOUSE

What's sexier than a bad boy? A badass man who's got his shit together.

Max Alexander is nearing thirty-five. He's built a successful company and conquered the business world, but he's never been lucky in love. Focusing so much time on his business and raising his daughter, adulting has come at the expense of his personal life.

His social skills are shit, his patience is shot, and at times, his temper runs hot.

The last thing he has time for is the recently single, too-gorgeous-for-her-own-good young woman he hires to take care of his little girl. She's a distraction he doesn't need, and besides, there's no way she'd be interested.

But you know what they say about assumptions?

Acknowledgments

I would like to thank my dedicated team for helping this book come to life, each in your own way. A big thank-you and a tackle-hug to these fabulous ladies: Danielle Sanchez, Natasha Madison, Meghan March, Pam Berehulke, Beverly Tubb, Amy Bosica, Sara Eirew, Rachel Brookes, and last but not least, Franci Neill.

An immense amount of gratitude goes to my readers. I love writing about all the bumps in the road on the way to a happily-ever-after, and I'm so thankful that you love reading about them. Let's never break up, okay?

I would like to thank my family for standing by my side and supporting my dreams, no matter how "out there" they might have seemed. Of those, my husband is my biggest and best supporter, and my rock. He believes wholeheartedly that I can do anything I set my mind to. I know I don't deserve his never-ending love and devotion, but I'm so thankful for it.

About the Author

A *New York Times*, *Wall Street Journal*, and *USA TODAY* bestselling author of more than twenty titles, Kendall Ryan has sold more than a million e-books, and her books have been translated into several languages in countries around the world. She's a traditionally published author with Simon & Schuster and Harper Collins UK, as well as an independently published author.

Since she first began self-publishing in 2012, she's appeared at #1 on Barnes & Noble and iBooks charts around the world. Her books have also appeared on the *New York Times* and *USA TODAY* bestseller list more than two dozen times. Ryan has been featured in such publications as *USA TODAY*, *Newsweek*, and *In Touch Weekly*.

Website: www.kendallryanbooks.com

Facebook: Kendall Ryan Books

Twitter: @kendallryan1

Other Books by Kendall Ryan

Made in the USA
San Bernardino, CA
09 February 2017